SEVEN SACKS *of* RICE

and other baggage

NICHOLAS YONG

An earlier version of "The Queen Of Heaven" was published in
A View Of Stars by Marshall Cavendish (2021).

Text © Nicholas Yong

Published in 2023 by Marshall Cavendish Editions
An imprint of Marshall Cavendish International

All rights reserved

No part of this publication may be reproduced, stored in a retrieval system or
transmitted, in any form or by any means, electronic, mechanical, photocopying,
recording or otherwise, without the prior permission of the copyright owner.
Requests for permission should be addressed to the Publisher, Marshall Cavendish
International (Asia) Private Limited, 1 New Industrial Road, Singapore 536196.
Tel: (65) 6213 9300.
E-mail: genref@sg.marshallcavendish.com
Website: www.marshallcavendish.com

The publisher makes no representation or warranties with respect to the contents
of this book, and specifically disclaims any implied warranties or merchantability
or fitness for any particular purpose, and shall in no event be liable for any loss
of profit or any other commercial damage, including but not limited to special,
incidental, consequential, or other damages.

Other Marshall Cavendish Offices:
Marshall Cavendish Corporation, 800 Westchester Ave, Suite N-641, Rye Brook,
NY 10573, USA • Marshall Cavendish International (Thailand) Co Ltd, 253 Asoke,
16th Floor, Sukhumvit 21 Road, Klongtoey Nua, Wattana, Bangkok 10110, Thailand
• Marshall Cavendish (Malaysia) Sdn Bhd, Times Subang, Lot 46, Subang Hi-Tech
Industrial Park, Batu Tiga, 40000 Shah Alam, Selangor Darul Ehsan, Malaysia

Marshall Cavendish is a registered trademark of Times Publishing Limited

National Library Board, Singapore Cataloguing in Publication Data
Name(s): Yong, Nicholas.
Title: Seven sacks of rice : and other baggage / Nicholas Yong.
Description: Singapore : Marshall Cavendish Editions, 2023.
Identifier(s): ISBN 978-981-5084-58-0 (paperback)
Subject(s): LCSH: Families--Singapore--Fiction. | Short stories, Singaporean
(English)
Classification: DDC S823--dc23

Printed in Singapore

For Gillian

For Mother and Ah Ma

Contents

Seven Sacks of Rice	7
The Other Family	24
Ming Chao	41
The Woodcutter	62
The Chicken Task Force	82
Water Body	99
The Runner	116
The Queen of Heaven	136
Heightened Alert	147
Mr Kim	166
Acknowledgements	182
About the Author	184

Seven Sacks of Rice

Lee Kim Choo stood alone at the edge of the clearing and waited. It was almost first light.

Her two cousins had helped carry the gunny sacks for several kilometres through the forest before walking off, leaving her there with the load. Kim Choo was clammy with sweat but as the heat of her exertions gradually faded, the cold seeped into her bones, leaving her shivering. After so many years in Nanyang, she was unaccustomed to the weather back home.

The woman Kim Choo had come to meet lived in the next village, and was known to her only by Lee, her family name. Lee had insisted they gather here, far from where they lived and at an ungodly hour. Perhaps it was down to a lingering sense of shame. In any case, Kim Choo had no desire to see her again once their business was concluded.

The woman emerged from the woods accompanied by two men, clutching a large cloth bundle in her arms. Her eyes were puffy and drawn, for she had been arguing with her husband and children all night. The quarrel had only ended when she asked, "So which one of you will volunteer not to eat?"

Kim Choo cast a glance at the sacks at her feet. Each of them reached up to waist height and weighed around 25 kilograms. They had cost her a small fortune, and would take years to repay. Lee had originally wanted eight sacks of rice. Kim Choo bargained it down to seven.

Without a word, the woman placed the bundle in Kim Choo's arms. She and the two men picked up the sacks and left. Only a keen observer would have noticed the slightest hesitation in her stride as she walked away.

Kim Choo opened the bundle. Inside was a rosy-cheeked little boy, fast asleep and curled up against the cold. She frowned, for the boy's mouth was lopsided. The woman had not told her.

But she beamed as she walked away. Now the family was complete.

There are no living witnesses to the events that unfolded in Chaozhou more than 70 years ago but this much is known: Like so many other Chinese emigrants, Lee Kim Choo and Koh Hee Cheng had arrived in Singapore in the 1930s in search of a better life. Sometime in January 1949, the couple decided to return to China for good, and brought their four daughters from Singapore back to his home village in Chaozhou, in the Chaoshan region of China. Hee Cheng's mother had died and the family needed them. At that point, Kim Choo had had no sons despite multiple attempts and multiple miscarriages. Like many Chinese women of her generation – she was born in 1915 – she longed for a baby boy, for sons still meant everything. So, during Kim Choo's time back in China, she bought a four-year-old boy from an impoverished family with too many children, and later brought him to Singapore. He cost seven sacks of rice, one less than what his birth mother had asked for.

Here is the story of the boy who was traded for rice, his adoptive sisters who loved him and the mother who carried the ache of his rejection in her heart forever.

Liak Eng is the youngest of Kim Choo's four daughters, and has two younger brothers. There is also an adopted brother called Ming Ching. Among Kim Choo's grandchildren, almost none had ever met this uncle. All they knew was that he wanted nothing to do with the family. They came to think of him as a mythical creature, like a pontianak or a water spirit, that everyone has heard of but never actually seen.

The grandchildren remember Kim Choo as a wizened old woman with kindly eyes, invariably dressed in what to their young minds were pyjamas. Spry and alert, with a faintly musty smell, she would beam at her grandsons and joyfully call them "hao seh kia", for they were all fine young men to her. She would cook beh cai tng (cabbage soup with fishballs) for the children, accompanied by eggs, rice and liberal amounts of soy sauce. Every now and then, she made png kueh, steamed rice dumplings shaped like a pink teardrop and stuffed with rice and dried shrimp, with sweet sauce drizzled all over them.

Kim Choo was fond of listening to Teochew operas on the radio and playing Chap Ji Kee, a lottery game of placing bets while guessing a number from a set of 12. Her eventual decline started with a stroke that weakened the left side of her body, and accelerated with the onset of dementia that saw her constantly buying braised duck for the family, as if it was still her responsibility to cook. As she declined, she was reduced to sitting in her rocking chair all day long. She would occasionally soil herself, leaving an exasperated Liak Eng and the young Indonesian helper she employed to clean her up. By the end, she couldn't tell her grandsons apart.

It wasn't always like that. In her prime, the grandchildren adored her because she loved them the way she had never loved her own children. As Liak Eng once derisively told her sons, "She had many grandsons by then and she was content. She wasn't nice to us before that."

In the 1950s, long before the rise of the multi-storey HDB blocks, Kim Choo and Hee Cheng's family lived in a kampung in Pukat Road, which was located off River Valley Road. In the old days, there were few flush toilets, so everyone shared a common toilet: an outhouse with a bucket. The night soil man would go around every morning collecting and emptying the buckets for a fee. Everyone paid their share, but for reasons no one could recall, Kim Choo decided not to pay the fee one day. This resulted in a scuffle with a female neighbour – while she was heavily pregnant with her youngest son, no less – which only ended when one of her daughters pulled the neighbour's hair and wouldn't let go until she relented.

Kim Choo's fury was often directed at her husband and her children. She doted on the grandchildren. But she never did talk about the lost uncle.

Liak Eng was born in Singapore in December 1948. She was later told that while her neighbours and relatives rejoiced at the birth of a fourth child and threw a party, her mother locked herself in her room and wept. It was not the boy Kim Choo had wanted so badly.

Shortly after she turned a month old, Hee Cheng brought his wife and children back to Chaozhou. It took them a week to sail there in a junk. The couple had been brought together by an arranged marriage when she was 16 and he 21. In Singapore, they both sold clothes at different locations. They quarrelled often, especially as Hee Cheng was an inveterate gambler, and they struggled to make ends meet with so many children. But they planned to start a new life back in China.

Then the People's Republic of China was proclaimed on 1 October 1949.

History tells us that some 1.2 million people fled the mainland for Taiwan as the forces of the Chinese Communist Party closed in. Many parts of China were caught up in the upheaval of the times, and Chaoshan was no exception. Hee Cheng ended up fleeing back to Singapore on his own, for the People's Liberation Army was looking for conscripts and offered rewards to those who turned in eligible men.

But he did something inexplicable as well: he took the

family's entry permits, which served in lieu of passports back then, with him when he left. No one truly knows why. But for a man in his 30s with a wife and four children to support, it must have been a chance to regain his freedom.

So Kim Choo was left to fend for herself with four young girls, the eldest of whom was only 10. Amid the turmoil of the nascent years of the PRC, they ended up staying in Chaozhou for four years.

Life was hard and food was scarce in 1950s China. The five of them were squeezed into a hut that was also used to house pigs. Even though they were peasants like everyone else, the family was regarded as foreigners and treated with suspicion. If they happened to have an extra portion of potatoes, it was best to keep it hidden. In the Communist worldview, anyone with even vaguely capitalist associations could be easily construed as an enemy of the state.

The couple had far more worldly concerns beyond political ideology. One day, Hee Cheng wrote to his wife: since she couldn't bear a son, she should buy one, so that the Koh family name could carry on. So she asked around and purchased a boy, as easily as you might go to the market and buy some vegetables. Her husband named him Ming Ching, or Ming Shen in hanyu pinyin. His hope was that the boy would leave a deep impression on those he met.

But the Kohs were still stuck in China, sans the husband and father who should have been their provider and protector. Kim Choo chafed at being treated like a second-class citizen by villagers and officials alike. She didn't help matters by dressing in the colourful clothes she had brought from Singapore, that attracted stares and snide whispers from the neighbours. It did not pay to stand out with informers and meddlesome party officials all around. But she could not care less about what other people thought. Kim Choo said what she thought and did as she pleased, even if it brought on a world of unnecessary trouble.

Eventually, Kim Choo had enough. She got someone to write to her husband's sister, who chided Hee Cheng and shamed him into sending them their travel permits.

But how were they to bring their new son back to Singapore? The records, even as primitive as they were at the time, showed that Lee Kim Choo had brought four children with four travel permits to China. How was she to explain the fifth child once she got off the boat, when she and her husband had been apart for four years, much less get a fifth permit for him?

Hee Cheng concocted a scheme that sounds ridiculous in its simplicity now. He told his wife to dress Ming Ching up as a girl, in order to pass him off as one of their daughters.

Then Kim Choo left China with the boy, leaving Liak Eng in Chaozhou in the boy's place.

Liak Eng, aged four at the time, can't remember a thing about it now. Liak Eng's sisters tell her that their mother had instructed her to go and change her clothes, and they left while she did so. For the rest of their lives, Kim Choo's own children resented her for what she did.

"She left a daughter there and bought a son. It's not right," Lee Eng, the second eldest of the sisters, said once. "We were very angry with her."

They left China in February 1953. Five months later, Hee Cheng came up with another idea. His wife remained illiterate all her life, but he had taught himself to read and followed current events closely. Hee Cheng helped a woman from his village to apply for a visa to China, as she wanted to see her relatives. In exchange, she brought along Liak Eng's entry permit and used it to bring her home.

The sisters burst into tears when they saw their youngest sibling again. She had been left in the care of Hee Cheng's uncle's wife, who had not even bothered to shower her. There were pimples all over her face and she was thin as a rake, for she had refused to drink milk. She looked like she had been living on the streets. But Liak Eng was home.

That wasn't the case for Ming Ching, who would sit in a corner of the family's attap hut and repeat again and again in Teochew, "This is not my home."

"Ming Ching, where are you?"

The entire kampung had been mobilised to search for the runaway boy, with Kim Choo at the head of the search party. She was drenched in sweat and worried sick. Ming Ching had gone missing again, and it was already close to midnight. The neighbours traipsed through the nearby forest and streets and alleyways with torchlights for hours, but to no avail. Their shouts echoed through the air, and still the boy was nowhere to be seen.

Kim Choo's husband was blithely dismissive. "Let him go," he said through a haze of cigarette smoke. "Why bother searching for him? He doesn't want to be a part of this family."

Her reply was brief. "I paid seven sacks of rice for him."

A sudden shout from one of the neighbours brought Kim

Choo scurrying. There he was, a small thing crouching in a drain. He squinted in the glare of the multiple torchlights aimed at him. A wave of relief washed over her.

"Ming Ching, what are you doing?" cried Kim Choo. "Be a good boy and come home with Mama." She reached out her hand to him.

But Ming Ching didn't move. He hugged his knees to his chest and buried his face in them. Try as she might, his adoptive mother could not get him out of the drain.

Even today, more than seven decades on, the fact that she was left behind haunts Liak Eng. "Imagine if something had happened to me, and I could not come home," she mused out loud one evening. "I would still be in China today."

She would never have met her husband either, nor given birth to her two sons. With the turmoil that China underwent from the middle of the century, from the Great Leap Forward to the Cultural Revolution, she might not even be alive today.

Liak Eng was an outlier among her sisters in that she made up her mind to go to school in the 1950s, at a time when girls were told that education was unnecessary. It was a message that her mother repeated ad nauseum too, one which her other daughters took on board. The only reason she assented to Liak Eng's request was that at the time, the colonial authorities were encouraging girls to get an education. For every girl who was sent to school, families were rewarded with the princely sum of $10.

A kindly neighbour, whom Liak Eng considers an angel sent to help her, also urged Kim Choo to send her to a primary school where the medium of instruction was English, so that it would be easier to find a job in the future. In the years when Singapore's independence was still far off, this turned out to be prescient. The neighbour never stopped helping her. Once, when it was pouring, she picked Liak Eng up and carried her home on piggyback in the rain. Liak Eng ended up completing her O-levels, an uncommon achievement in the 1960s, and becoming a teacher for the next four decades.

Why was a seven-year-old girl so determined to go to school? In all probability, Liak Eng inherited her father's intellect and her mother's stubbornness. And perhaps knowing that her life could have been vastly different lit a fire in her.

Unlike Liak Eng, there was to be no happy ending for Ming Ching, nor any angels to pick him up. She remembers her adopted brother as a dour boy who never had much to say. It certainly didn't help that Hee Cheng, who was the one who had told his wife to buy a son, took an immediate dislike to him. Nor that, when instructed to help deliver goods by bicycle to Hee Cheng's store, he would go missing for days on end. Hee Cheng beat the boy and locked him in a room when he incurred his displeasure, and bent his thumb when he didn't hold his chopsticks properly. The anger that the sisters felt at their mother for abandoning Liak Eng may have spilled over to their treatment of him too.

He ran away from home time and again. On occasion, he would be found sleeping by roadside stalls. It got to the point where Lee Eng asked her mother to send him back to China, but Kim Choo merely repeated her stock line, "I paid seven sacks of rice for him." She was always the first one to look for him whenever he went missing. Eventually, the day came when Ming Ching did not come home, and his adoptive family stopped searching for him. He was 12 years old.

As it turned out, Kim Choo gave birth to her first son a couple of years after Ming Ching came to Singapore. Another boy followed suit in due course. Kim Choo doted on the two boys that she had longed for all her life. And yet, the pain of her adopted son's absence never went away.

Kim Choo would never have put it in those terms, but she loved Ming Ching. He was very much her first son, but he never did regard himself as her child. Ming Ching couldn't stop thinking of his birth mother. He pined for her as he went to sleep each night in an unfamiliar house surrounded by strangers. And when he realised that he was never going home again, he gave up on his adoptive family completely.

In the process, Ming Ching gave up on life itself.

Liak Eng came to empathise with, if not to understand, what her mother did. Besides struggling so long to have sons – who ultimately let her down – Kim Choo and Hee Cheng were poor for most of their lives. They had seven children to support, and Hee Cheng's proclivities did not help. More than once, he lost the household money on gambling. This resulted in volcanic outbursts of temper from his wife. At times, she would kick her husband awake in order to berate him for not working harder.

There was another child too that Kim Choo never spoke of. Before Ming Ching was adopted and before the family went to China, she did give birth to a baby boy. But after several months, he became deathly ill with fever, and she took him to a hospital. He was on the verge of death when she left him there, so Kim Choo never went back for him. She reasoned that he was unlikely to survive, so there was no point in enquiring after him. Perhaps she had grown calluses on her heart, after enduring so much pain.

No one knows if the baby boy survived, but Liak Eng and her siblings did not stop trying to reach out to the brother who was very much alive and present. He never did reach his hand out to them in return.

Ming Ching would vanish whenever one of the family ran into him. Lee Eng once saw him in Chinatown, where he was working as a cobbler. The next time she went there, he was gone. This happened repeatedly. One week he was a security guard, the next a hawker's assistant. At other times, he would turn up as a cleaner, or a supermarket worker. Every time he was spotted, he quit his job and moved to another location. His adoptive sisters constantly asked him to come home, to no avail.

The last time Lee Eng saw Ming Ching was more than 10 years ago. Was it at Ngee Ann City, where he worked as a cleaner? Or was it at the Sheng Siong outlet somewhere in Tanglin Halt? She cannot recall anymore. The years get mixed up and the details blur, until Ming Ching gets further and further away.

The middle-aged man sweeping the ground outside the shopping mall didn't see his sister at first. Dark clouds were gathering, but the humidity never went away. He wiped the sweat off his brow with a ragged towel as he proceeded along. His clothes were grimy and stained, and had been patched up more than once. It was two days since Christmas Eve, and still the cleaners were sweeping up confetti and packet drinks and burst balloons.

Exhausted, he took a seat on a nearby bench. He had dreamt of his mother the night before. He was a child again, and she was holding him close to her breast, wrapped in a cloth bundle. He knew that they were on their way home. He felt safe, comforted. But in the next instant, he was alone in the middle of the forest. He cried out for her, but she was nowhere to be seen.

He could never quite visualise his mother's face when he was awake. All that came to mind were passing glimpses of her. The way she wore her hair in a tight bun. Her rolling gait as she took him to the market on piggyback, with the other children in tow. The smell of her sweat as she came home from a long day of work in the fields. A lullaby that she would sing to lull him to sleep, the words of which he could never recall.

Whenever he awoke from a dream of his mother, he would screw his eyes shut and concentrate, grasping at the most minute details and desperately trying to commit them to memory. But they fell away rapidly, like water in the palm of his hand. She could have appeared before him and he would not have recognised her. Did she ever think of him, he wondered.

A shadow fell over him. He turned his head upwards, and stiffened.

"Hello, Second Sister," he said.

Lee Eng had just knocked off work and gone to buy dinner before heading home, which was a long bus ride away. But she recognised that familiar profile at once, even from a distance.

Lee Eng took in his appearance and winced. His complexion was even darker than the last time she saw him, a testament to his constant toil in the sun. He was skinnier too, and he reeked of cigarette smoke. But his mouth was as crooked as ever, and her estranged brother still carried the same dour disposition, like that of a child who was perpetually bullied.

"How are you, Ming Ching?"

"I am fine."

"You're so thin. Are you eating enough?"

"I'm all right."

"Did you get into a fight?" Lee Eng pointed to the long scar on his arm, which must have been inflicted recently. He waved off her question dismissively.

"Where are you living now?" He didn't respond. Instead, he got up and resumed sweeping the ground, moving away from her. She followed him.

"Did you know that Ah Beh died?"

"Yes. Tong Min told me."

"You talk to Dua Hiah?"

"Sometimes."

"Why didn't you come to the funeral?"

"I don't attend funerals."

Lee Eng sighed. She knew that she could not change his mind, but at least she could buy him dinner. She was sure that he needed it.

"Take care, Second Sister," he said before she could speak. He gave one last glance at her and walked off, broomstick in hand.

As they parted, Lee Eng knew that she would not see him there again.

Liak Eng had been thinking about it for some time. She wanted to go and see her brother.

Lee Eng had heard that Ming Ching, who would be about 75 today, was working as a cleaner at a temple in Bishan. There was no way of knowing if he was still there, but Liak Eng wanted to try. "It would be good to see him before he dies," she told her sister.

The last time she saw him was in 2007, when she happened upon him at a hawker centre in Kreta Ayer. They had not met in decades, but Liak Eng recognised that distinctive crooked mouth at once. She did not approach him but told her sisters about it. The siblings did not believe it until they went and saw for themselves. But they didn't speak to him, for fear that he would be frightened off again.

It was not some small, nondescript neighbourhood temple, as Liak Eng had thought. Instead, it was, as Google Maps labelled it, a "massive scenic Buddhist temple". The compound was reminiscent of a megachurch – it included prayer halls, a columbarium, a large canteen and a small secondhand goods store. The air was redolent with incense, and there were a great many monks and devotees coming to and fro.

Liak Eng stood in the foyer of the temple, unsure of where to go. She approached a masked monk in grey robes and explained the situation: she was trying to find a long-lost relative who might be residing at the temple as a cleaner. He said that that was not possible. "Our cleaning is outsourced." Nevertheless, the monk directed a young woman to bring her up to the HR office, where another staffer attended to her and carefully wrote Ming Ching's name down.

After a brief wait in a side room, she was told what she had been expecting: there was no record of him in the temple's database, which went back a decade. Even inquiries with the oldest staff members bore no fruit. No one had heard of an elderly cleaner with a lopsided mouth named Ming Ching.

But who knows if that was the truth? Maybe Ming Ching was really hiding in another room just round the corner, telling the staff in low tones not to let Liak Eng know that he was there. Or he was really the monk Liak Eng had spoken to, unrecognisable and inscrutable behind the mask, who recognised the sister that his fate was so closely intertwined with but would not acknowledge her. Or perhaps he was really to be found in the columbarium, his ashes residing in a niche alongside thousands of other long departed souls.

In the end, the simplest explanation will have to suffice: Ming Ching either left the temple long ago, or he had never resided there. He had vanished from the face of the earth, and there was no way of ever finding him.

When Liak Eng's eldest sister died recently, the family gathered for the wake to grieve together. That's what family is for, whatever your feelings towards them. For Ming Ching, he never saw them as kin, even though his sisters called him brother. As far as his adoptive siblings know, he never married and has no children either.

When Ming Ching dies, none of his family will be there. But perhaps he will be reunited with his biological family in the next world, or granted a new family to call his own. Maybe then he will find some measure of peace, and he can finally go home, and there will be no more need to run.

The Other Family

I was eight years old when I saw the other family for the first time.

There they were, a middle-aged Chinese couple with their two young children standing beside them as they sat on the kerusi hiasan, those tall wooden chairs with the ornately carved details paired with a small table between them. The chairs, placed just a few feet from the dining table, always reminded me of the kind seen at weddings, with their high backs and colourful cushions.

The radio was on, giving off the soft strains of M. Osman's "Suzana" as we sat down to dinner. Abah had a rule that the TV, the old boxy kind with the aerial perched on top, had to be turned off at dinnertime, but he liked to have the radio playing softly. Every now and then, when an old song that they liked came on, Abah would turn up the volume and lead Mak into a dance, which delighted us.

The four of them assessed us dispassionately as my mother dished out generous helpings of nasi and ayam masak merah, along with the sambal kangkong. They appeared to have stepped out of the 1960s, with that decade's clothing and hairstyles. I could never quite describe them until I watched *Growing Up* years later and realised that they were dressed exactly like those characters. They stared at us, hushed and unmoving, and I stared back until I could stand it no longer and turned away.

I pulled on my mother's sleeve. "Mak?"

"Yes, sayang?"

"Those people are watching us."

"What people?"

"The four people there, at the chairs."

My mother started, the colour gradually fading from her cheeks. "There's no one there, sayang."

I turned to where they continued gazing at us blankly.

"But they're right there."

We moved into a HUDC flat in Jurong East in the 1990s. The government said HUDC flats were meant for the aspiring sandwich class: Singaporeans who wanted more than a HDB dwelling, but couldn't quite afford a house. My father worked in the shipping line and slaved away for years so that we could move into one.

It was huge, not like the puny BTOs they churn out these days. Besides the master bedroom, living room and kitchen, there were two more rooms and a study. It felt like a castle, all 158 square metres of it. I would run round and round the flat, from the living room to the split level below to the master bedroom and back, the folds of my baju butterfly trailing behind me.

I can still recall exactly how it looked. The walls were painted a light shade of green, and overhanging the living room was a framed Ayatul Kursi, the 255th verse of the second chapter of the Quran, rendered in beautiful calligraphy. The dining table had linen emblazoned with illustrations of fruits and vegetables, as well as white lace paper doily place settings. On one of the walls hung a giant fork and spoon, the accessory of choice for every self-respecting Malay household. The furniture was all wooden and handmade, none of that mass produced rubbish everyone seems to like so much these days.

Taking pride of place in the living room was the kerusi pak awang, that three-seater sofa made of jati wood and imported from Indonesia, and which came in a set with hard cushions, a coffee table and two single-seater armchairs. My parents went to great lengths to clean and polish that sofa and its accoutrements because it was one of the first things they had bought when they got married. And of course, the coffee table – and just about every bare surface – was covered by crochet covers with intricate patterns.

The only place that was out of step with the rest of the flat was the kitchen, which was decorated with gorgeous handmade Moroccan tiles. Mak had read a travel book about Morocco years ago and it was her dream holiday destination. She never did make it there, since she was so busy with household duties. By the time we were all grown up, her knees were worn out and her lust for travel had dimmed.

We lived there for almost a decade and it's been more than 20 years since we moved out. It was the place where my sisters – Aishah and Yasmin – and I played and had birthday parties and gossiped about the boys we liked. And for as long as we lived there, I was the only one who could see the unwanted guests in our midst.

In retrospect, it should have been clear from the start that something wasn't quite right with our home.

When my parents first bought it, there was an altar to the Virgin Mary in the living room. There was nothing unusual about that and it didn't bother us much, since the Quran teaches that Mariam is the greatest woman who ever lived, may Allah be pleased with her. We gave the altar away to some Catholic friends and proceeded with the usual blessing of the flat by an ustaz. However, while the contractors were renovating, they discovered little crosses embedded deep in the back of every cupboard, even the ones in the kitchen. I'm not sure if it ever occurred to my parents to ask why the last people to live there felt that was necessary.

You might be thinking that I had an overactive imagination as a child, or that I just wanted attention. But from the time I was very young, it was my relatives who said that I was the most sensitive to the presence of benda halus, the invisible spirits that were trapped between the natural world and the nether world. They said that I had mata batin – the inner eye. I believe it was my grandmother's domestic helper who first pointed it out. She came from the Indonesian island of Madura, a place said to be known for black magic. The first time she set eyes on me, she told my grandmother, "Kalau Aatika dilahir di kampung saya, dia pasti dipilih untuk menjadi dukun." If Aatika had been born in my village, she would have been chosen to be a shaman.

This nearly caused Mak Tok to fall out of her rocking

chair. My grandmother sent her packing soon enough. For the longest time after, whenever Mak Tok experienced any sort of misfortune or inconvenience, she would mumble to herself, "Si dia tu ada tinggalkan benda ke." She must have put a curse on me.

My relatives certainly took the helper at her word. Mak tells me that my aunts and uncles would bring me along to view property that they were thinking of buying. According to her, if I was well behaved and my normal self, they would know that the place was, in their words, "clean". On the other hand, if I bawled for no reason – and I very rarely did that even as a toddler – they would quickly make their excuses, scoop me up and leave. The running joke among my relatives was that I was their "free ghost detector".

I certainly proved my worth to my third aunt and her husband. She brought me along for a viewing where, according to her, I threw up when I crossed the threshold and shivered uncontrollably. Her husband dismissed it all as "superstitious nonsense" and they went ahead and bought the place and moved in. But the lights in the apartment started blinking non-stop, which resulted in repeated calls to the electrician, who could never find anything wrong. Their cat Rania would often hiss at something invisible in the corner, her back arched as if ready to attack. The final straw came when a heavy piece of the ceiling fell abruptly and almost hit their toddler. They sold that flat in a hurry.

You might ask yourself why any parent would casually subject their offspring to this sort of trauma, but well, it was the 1990s. Kids were expected to toughen up, not talk about their feelings. I suppose it's also easier to deal with the supernatural when it's not in your backyard. When there are trespassers in your own home, it's much harder not to care.

After that first time, I saw the four intruders – or were we the real intruders to them? – on multiple occasions. The parents would either be there with the kids, or on their own. Without exception, they wore the same vacant faces as they inspected us from their perch on the chairs my parents loved so much. They were practically a part of the furniture.

I could never bring myself to make eye contact with them. From time to time, I would pluck up the courage to fix my gaze on them just a bit longer. Were they angry with us, or did they need help? Where had they come from? What was it that they wanted? I was dying to ask them these questions, and to hear a response. I would lie awake at night, tossing and turning beneath my blanket. I wanted to voice these queries out loud, but I was terrified that they might hear me and appear in my room without warning.

Yet, all they ever really did was sit on those chairs and stare.

"Mak, I can see them again," was my constant refrain to my parents. I begged them to remove the chairs. I promised to do all my homework, go to bed on time every night, give up sweets, anything. No matter what I said, they didn't believe me. Or should I say, they didn't want to believe me.

"Don't talk nonsense," my mother would firmly declare. *Abah*, who has always been a man of immense faith, did believe me, I think, but took a different tack. We had lived in many places over the years, and with every new home, he would move in by himself a few days before us, when he made sure to say his prayers in every room. It was his way of showing that he was not afraid of anything that might be dwelling there. "We are the special creation of Allah," he would declare. "What do we have to fear from jinns and spirits?"

Maybe he was right. But he wasn't the one who had to deal with people eyeballing him as if he was the one who didn't belong.

Time passed in our castle. We settled into life there and got on with whatever we were busy with. My sisters and I had school, my father worked long hours and my mother was busy running the home. The other family faded into the background. Almost.

Even when the invisible ones did not materialise, small incidents reminded us that they were never far away. Objects like a pair of scissors or a nail clipper would go missing, only to turn up somewhere else entirely, like at the bottom of a pile of freshly laundered clothes. Doors would suddenly become locked, only to be magically unlocked hours later.

Most frightening of all, my sisters and I discovered foreign currency in the most random of places. I would reach into my pocket and come up with old Chinese coins or British shillings. Aishah, our eldest sister, might be reading a book when a ringgit note would fall out of it. This was at a time when our family did not go on holidays, not even to Malaysia. The only one who travelled was Abah, who went to Indonesia regularly for work. Yet we never found any rupiah.

One day, I returned from school and no one else was home. I settled myself down on the floor of the living room at the split level, not bothering to change out of my uniform. I had a habit of lying on my stomach between the TV console and the coffee table while reading the newspapers. My parents gave me so much grief about keeping the sofa clean and not eating on it that I gave up and took to the floor instead.

I remember it so clearly. It was a cloudy day with no breeze. At that age, I didn't really read the papers. I just liked flipping through them and scanning the photos. It made me feel all grown up. Whenever I spotted a familiar word or discovered a new one, I would memorise it so that I could ask Abah about it later. It pleased him to see me taking the initiative to learn new things.

I was turning the pages when, all at once, the newspapers took flight, as if someone had grabbed hold of them and flung them in the air. I jumped up and screamed. In the glass panels of the TV console, I could see the reflection of a child's legs running past. I heard something else too. It was a child giggling.

I ran to my room and locked myself in, diving under the blanket despite the heat. When Mak and Abah came back an hour later, I ran to them in tears, drenched in sweat, and wouldn't let go of my mother. When they finally calmed me down, I told them what had happened, gulping every five words or so as I was crying so hard.

I'll never forget what my mother said when I had finished

my story. "Aatika, don't make up stories like that." Try as she might to project an air of serenity, there was an unmistakable note of fear in her voice.

I graduated from primary school, while my sisters were about to finish secondary school and university. I had given up on telling my parents about the sightings, since they never took me seriously. I tried my best to ensure that I was never alone at home.

I remember the incident that finally convinced Mak, for all her denials, that I was telling the truth. Yasmin and I loved completing large jigsaw puzzles, the kind with a thousand pieces or more. I have always been close to Yasmin, my middle sister, since we are only a few years apart in age, unlike Aishah who is 10 years older than me. We spent hours and hours working on those puzzles. It was a special treat when Abah returned from another work trip with a new one. Whatever we were doing, Yasmin and I would jump up and literally snatch it from his grasp, before ripping the box open and starting on it immediately. It took immense patience and effort to complete those puzzles, and the joy we derived from it was almost euphoric. Our parents were grateful for our shared passion, because it meant that for just a while, we weren't making any noise. It amused Abah to no end. "My daughters love jigsaw puzzles more than me," he would say.

Our latest project was an epic one – a bewitching image of the sprawling Iguazu Falls, located between Brazil and Argentina. It consisted of 2,000 pieces, and Yasmin and I worked on it for over a month. When we weren't at school or doing our homework, we were piecing the puzzle together. If one of us wasn't around, she would wait for the other. I'm not sure if I've ever been this dedicated to anything else in my life, not even my own child.

Days and weeks went by, and we were near the end. That was when we discovered that we were three pieces short. This had never happened before, so we naturally assumed that we had misplaced them. We searched high and low, yet they were nowhere to be found. Mak was a neat freak who took immense pride in keeping her home clean, with everything spick and span and precisely where it should be. Even with her regular sweeping and mopping, she could not find them. In the end, we put the puzzle away and got on with other things.

One day, my mother let out a scream that was so loud, all the neighbours must have heard it. We came rushing out of our rooms to find her standing aghast at the threshold of the master bedroom.

"Sayang, tell me the truth. Did you put this here?" She pointed to the floor where three puzzle pieces were neatly laid out in a line. Examining them carefully, I realised that they were the missing pieces of our Iguazu Falls puzzle.

"Mak! How did you find them?"

"Did you put this here?" She repeated her question with an anger that was palpable.

"No, I never," I protested. My sisters were standing around, not saying a word. I could sense how frightened they were.

"Jangan bohong!"

"I never!"

"Don't lie!"

"Why you don't believe me, Mak?" The tears of frustration and anger flowed freely. I had never seen my mother like that before. She didn't say another word. She merely stood there, frozen to the spot. And the more I took in her terrified expression, the more I realised that she knew I was telling the truth.

Do you recall *Love 2000*, the super popular TV drama series that came out at the height of the Japanese wave? It's the one with the ridiculously handsome Takeshi Kaneshiro playing, of all things, a secret agent sent to infiltrate the Japanese foreign ministry. Yasmin and I were in our mid-teens when it came out. Believe it or not, you actually had to tune in to a TV channel at a specific time every week in order to watch an episode of the TV series you were following. If you couldn't make it and didn't manage to record it on your VCR, that was it. You had to make do with an episode summary from *8 Days* if you wanted to know what had happened. Young people don't know how good they have it now. Yes, I know I sound like my parents.

Anyway, we swooned over Takeshi and tuned in faithfully every week. Yasmin and I were like a tag team, reminding each other on Sundays when it was airing. Notwithstanding the laughable premise and a lead character who would have been exposed on his first day on the job, it also had a soundtrack that we loved. We went to HMV to get it and practically wore out the CD with our incessant playing, as we plugged in to Yasmin's Discman with shared earphones. My favourite track was "Forbidden Love", the piano instrumental theme by Reuben Wong. We would go through the lyric sleeve and memorise the Japanese lyrics, even though we had no idea what they meant, and sing along together.

The fad passed. Yasmin and I moved on to other TV shows and boy bands and the next craze. But there came a lazy Sunday afternoon when we were lounging around with nothing to do, when Yasmin pulled the soundtrack out of her CD collection. She caught my eye and we both giggled. Without another word, she took out her Discman and inserted the CD. She frowned as she took in the lyric sleeve, which was worn out from multiple folding and refolding. "Eh. How come now the lyrics in English?"

"Apa?"

"See. All English." She proffered the sleeve to me. I flipped through it and realised that she was right.

"Did you mix it up with another CD?"

"No leh. It's correct, it's the right cover." The sleeve was indeed that of the *Love 2000* soundtrack, but the lyrics didn't make any sense. They seemed more like a collection of random English words, with no resemblance to the Japanese lyrics we had pored over endlessly.

"Never mind, let's just play the CD." I took out the earphones, handed one end to Yasmin and pressed play. I closed my eyes as the hum of the spinning CD took hold and prepared for the comforting notes of "Forbidden Love".

For the first time in my life, I felt chills in my body.

I opened my eyes and turned to my sister. Her expression

told me that I wasn't just imagining things.

We frantically skipped through every track on the CD. We must have taken it out and examined it at length at least a dozen times, before popping it back into the Discman and playing it again. No matter what we did, there was no trace of our beloved *Love 2000* album, but just the same thing playing again and again. It was the sound of children warbling incomprehensibly, long and slow and mournful. It reminded me of old-fashioned Christian hymns I had heard in school.

We never played that CD again. Yasmin couldn't bear to throw it away, as CDs were an expensive luxury with our teenage allowances. Instead, she hid it at the back of a shelf behind some books, as we each pretended that it didn't exist.

We didn't tell our parents either. By then, we had learned not to mention such incidents to Mak. It would only upset her.

I stood in the middle of the flat, tentative and uncertain.

"Hello? Are you there?"

It was our last day. The property had been sold to a young couple. Shockingly, not a word about the additional occupants had been said to them. Abah made a point of getting all of us together to recite surahs from the Quran in every room, every single day for a week.

"We must make sure this home is cleansed for the next residents," he told us, his tone so serious that it felt as if an ustaz was addressing us. Evidently, Abah had not considered that the new residents – nor the current ones – might not subscribe to the 5 Pillars of Islam, but I suppose the thought was there.

I recall my parents informing us over dinner that they had accepted an offer for the flat and found a new place, and that we would be moving out within months. Yasmin and I couldn't help giving each other knowing glances. I was about to ask them why when I noticed that Mak's gaze was fixed firmly on the dining table, and it remained that way throughout the meal. She was not her usual chatty self, and she was picking at her food. What would I have seen in her eyes if she had looked up? Might it have been the same expression she wore when she confronted me about the missing jigsaw puzzle pieces?

Most of the furniture had been removed, along with the Ayatul Kursi and the giant fork and spoon and the curtains. The ceiling fans and the TV console were still there, waiting to be dismantled and packed away. The movers had gone for lunch, while my parents were sorting things out at our new place. My sisters were with them, while I had been assigned to guard the old place as the last few bits and pieces were moved out. Our former home, now almost empty, echoed as I walked around.

I was 18 at the time, and about to graduate from junior college. As the years passed, I saw the other family less and less. There were fewer unexplained incidents too, much to our unspoken relief. They were a fading force, like the last vestiges of that fuzzy image you see on a television when you switch it off. It got to the point where I asked myself if I had somehow made up the whole thing. Perhaps my imagination really had taken over to the point where reality and fantasy became indistinguishable.

But I knew that they were real, and I never stopped thinking about them.

So on that final day, with just hours to go before we left forever, I finally worked up the courage to address them out loud. There was no answer.

My eyes fell on the kerusi hiasan, which had already been tightly wrapped in plastic for transport. I asked the question again. "Are you there?"

I waited and waited. Everything remained deathly still.

I felt silly. I felt guilty. Why had I waited so long to ask? What if they had simply needed help all this time, and I had just been oblivious and indifferent?

The seconds ticked by. I reflected on how we had never told anyone else about it, not even our relatives. On one occasion, I tried to tell my aunts and my mother shushed me, as if we were harbouring some shameful secret. Periodically, I would sit by myself at recess, lost in thought about the other family until the school bell went off. Once, a teacher came by and asked if I was all right. I had to resist the temptation to tell her that I lived in a haunted home. Instead, I just told her that I wanted to be alone. I think she was relieved that she didn't have to tell her head of department about me.

I began to weep. Even now, I can't explain why. It had been years, but I still could not bring myself to say what I really wanted to say.

"I wish," I said, stopping myself. I breathed in deeply and choked out the words. "I wish they could see you too."

That was when I felt a sudden gust of wind. For a split

second, I caught the legs of a child running past, reflected in the glass panels of the TV console, accompanied by soft, echoing giggles.

I never did find out where the other family came from. The closest I got to it was when I overheard two neighbours chatting about the fact that our block was known for suicides, and that a deranged couple who lived on the same floor as we did once threw their children down before jumping after them.

I have my own family now. My daughter Dianah is eight years old. She is the apple of my eye, and I beam at her the way Mak beams at me. My husband loves us quietly and fiercely, the way Abah did, though I have never told him about the spirits I grew up with. Life is good, and there is no need to bring up the past.

The other day, I was braiding Dianah's hair at the dining table when she pulled at my sleeve. "Mak?"

"Yes, sayang?" I was focused on the task at hand because I knew that Dianah liked her hair to be just right and would fuss endlessly about it.

"Who is that girl sitting on the sofa?"

I froze. She had said it so casually, as if she were pointing out a cat on the street, or a new toy she wanted.

"What girl?" I asked, my voice quivering.

"The one wearing the red dress." I braced myself and turned towards the couch. "There's no one there, Dianah."

"But she's there, Mak."

I continued braiding my daughter's hair, my hands moving mechanically back and forth. I thought back to my childhood and all those years I had spent trying to get my mother to believe me, and how awful it felt to see something that no one else could. I despaired that the curse of the mata batin had been passed on to the next generation and I blamed myself for it.

But I knew what to do next.

"Are you sure there's someone there, sayang?"

"Yes, Mak."

"Let's go say hello to her."

Ming Chao

The fat, plain, brown envelope appeared on the reporter's desk with the words "KIMBERLY NEO, THE NATIONAL TIMES" written with a black marker in neat handwriting, with no other markings, postage stamp or an address on it. Turning the envelope over gave no clue as to whom and where it had come from either. It may as well have materialised out of thin air.

Seated at her desk, Kim tucked a few loose strands of hair behind her ear and glared warily at the package. It had been placed on her external keyboard amid the piles of folders containing interview notes and other collateral that were neatly stacked all around her cubicle.

Kim turned her gaze upwards to take in the yellow and orange sticky notes, with reminders written in black caps like "READ YOUR STORY AT LEAST 3 TIMES" and "STORY MUST REFLECT THAT THE QUESTION WAS ASKED", that adorned the walls of her cubicle. Taking pride of place on the wall before her was a laminated list entitled "HAZEL TEO'S TOP 10 TIPS", a list of common grammatical errors compiled by a veteran editor who was the paper's grammar police. Unfortunately, Hazel had no advice on how to deal with anonymous parcels that mysteriously appeared on desks.

It was already evening, and despite the flexibility of work-from-home arrangements that meant only half the reporters were around, the familiar sounds and smells of the newsroom coming to life were taking over: journalists tapping away on their laptops, supervisors having discussions with subordinates in the open-concept meeting spaces, and editors poring over the early proofs of the next day's pages as their kopi sat steaming beside them. There was also a very slight whiff of body odour in the air, and Kim had a sickening feeling that at least part of it was coming from her. She could have filed her stories at home, but she didn't like writing alone with only the four walls for company.

Kim fervently hoped that the package wasn't from another one of those readers, like the one who had taken the time to send a handwritten note lambasting her interview with the celebrity who had found happiness with a third husband after two troubled marriages. "This cheap woman is only good for hooking a good man! You will only understand when you become a mother!" wrote the auntie. It was like a Facebook comment come to life, but with double the vitriol and half the intelligence. Kim could almost hear the hysteria coming off the page, delivered in piercing tones.

She dumped the note in the bottom drawer of her desk, along with all the other correspondence she had received from readers over the years. Maybe she would write a book someday.

Kim couldn't take her eyes off the envelope. Her workday

was nearly at an end, and she was planning to head home to prep for the next day's interview with a prominent CEO. There were also several stories pending for the weekend edition of the paper. But journalists are somewhat akin to the clueless teenagers in horror movies who head into a haunted building after being told not to: they just cannot resist the need to satisfy their curiosity.

It could also be another tip-off from an anonymous individual. God forbid, it might even be a note of appreciation from a reader. At a time when the paper was being roundly mocked by all and sundry for the abysmal quality of its articles – one online wag called it the government newsletter, except that actual newsletters were more interesting – some encouragement was sorely needed.

Kim's eyes flicked over to her watch. It was 5.45pm. I'm so going to regret this, she told herself as she picked up a penknife and slit the envelope open. She turned it upside down and shook the contents out vigorously. They landed on the desk with a soft thump. That was when she saw the thin, multi-coloured notes bearing the face of the Jade Emperor.

The scream she let out could be heard throughout the newsroom. "Fuck!" She sprung up from her chair and backed away from her desk.

Darren, her supervisor, came running over. "What's wrong? What's happened?"

Kim pointed to her desk, unable to even gaze upon it. Darren took a tentative step forward and saw the unmistakable hues of hell money. He broke into a wry grin and turned to the reporter.

"Are you going to buy us dinner?"

"Tell me again, please," said Jake as he adjusted his round wire-rimmed glasses and steepled his hands before his face.

It was almost 8.00pm. After the commotion of her colleagues crowding round her cubicle and trying to outdo one another with one-liners had died down, Darren packed up the notes and took Kim upstairs to Jacob Chan's office. The editor had summoned them after hearing the ruckus, and they were now seated around his desk, the dreaded package lying between them. It consisted of a fat stack of hell notes, several black-and-white photos and a handwritten letter. Kim couldn't stop fidgeting in her seat. All she wanted to do was go home and lie down. Nonetheless, she picked up the letter and read it out loud again for the benefit of the editor.

"Dear Kimberly, please tell the Prime Minister, I send you these incense money enough or not? You have earn so much yet you cannot give these elderly hawkering an income or this space to make a living. You and your ministers fully deserve these DEAD incense money. You must thank me for not teaching people to send you these ming chao," she read.

"Forgive me for interrupting. What's ming chao again?" asked Jake.

"Hell money," said Darren.

"I see. Please continue, Kim."

Kim resumed reading in the same flat monotone. It was all she could muster at this point. "There will be more of these type of letter and more incense money. On rainy day, you will be striked by lightning if you don't do anything."

She added, "He ends off with, 'We are not targeting you Kimberly, we are targeting the bastard PM. Please do something for Sungei.'"

Jake leaned back in his expensive gamer's chair, raised up to the maximum to make up for his lack of stature. A colleague once remarked to Kim that the editor reminded him of Pinocchio, whose one desire was to become a real boy. It wasn't difficult to see why. For all his attempts at projecting an air of friendliness and engaging in hail-fellow-well-met banter with the journalists, particularly when they bumped into one another in the threadbare pantry, his smile did not extend into his dead eyes. Jake unfailingly sought to project an amiable air, even though he often came across as unnerving more than anything else. Kim really wished he would stop trying to be friendly.

She had an uncomfortable sense that a deep well of anger resided within him, bubbling just beneath the tailored shirts and the immaculately trimmed hair with the hint of salt and pepper. There was a rumour that he had once harboured political ambitions, which were thwarted by the powers that be. There was no denying that he was immaculately groomed and dressed well. But as it was, the most complimentary description of Jake that Kim could think of was the one an analyst had used for an aspiring French presidential candidate: relatively inoffensive.

Jake picked up one of the photos and examined it at length, like a fine piece of art. It showed a young man standing before a roadside stall, beaming at the camera as he held a little boy in his arms. The boy, who was sucking on a lollipop, looked back at the camera curiously. Putting the photo down, he asked, "Do we know what exactly he is unhappy about?"

Darren chimed in. "I think it's about the Sungei Road market closure, Jake. Kim did a few stories and spoke to some of the affected hawkers. He's one of them." Popularly known as the Thieves Market, the flea market had seen vendors peddling their wares, mainly secondhand and vintage goods, and occasionally stolen items, in the Sungei Road area since the 1930s. They had survived numerous attempts to shut them down before the government closed the market for good a few months before, leaving hundreds of hawkers in the lurch. The resulting uproar from both hawkers and the public, which had grown nostalgic for all manner of things in recent years, left the authorities very nervous. Kim knew for a fact that they had pored over her stories and personally reached out to the vendors her articles quoted.

"Does he give his name?"

"It's signed 'Johnson Lee'. Assuming that's his real name lah," said Darren.

"Is the name familiar, Kim? Did you interview him?"

"Yes, Jake. He's been at the market since the fifties. He sells all kinds of junk, like old photos."

Kim was fascinated by the expression on Jake's face, as he pouted ever so slightly and squinted his eyes. Is he doing Blue Steel from *Zoolander*, she thought. His next query caught her off guard.

"Well, first of all, are you all right, Kim?"

Startled by the unexpected inquiry into her welfare from an editor, which was as rare as the threat she had just received,

Kim recovered quickly. "I'm okay, just in shock, I guess. I really shouldn't have opened that letter."

He put the photo down and adjusted his glasses again. "I've been doing this for a long time, Kim, and I have to tell you that threats from readers are not unusual at all in this newsroom. Fortunately, no one has ever made good on their threats."

"Okay, that's good."

"In this case, since the Prime Minister is involved, I am going to ask you to make a police report."

Kim was taken aback. "Is that really necessary, Jake? I mean, the hell notes are creepy lah, but he didn't really make a specific threat."

"Unfortunately, it is. I very much doubt if it's a serious threat, but I don't think we should take any chances. What do you have on for tomorrow?"

"I have a CEO interview."

"Darren, can you assign someone else to do it? And can I also trouble you to accompany Kim to the police station?"

"Of course, Jake."

Jake locked his eyes on Kim and tried his best to project empathy and kindness. "I am very sorry this happened to you, Kim. Why don't you take the day off tomorrow after you make the police report? You deserve a good rest."

"Thanks, Jake," said Kim wearily.

Kim awoke with a start. She had been having a nightmare in which she was sitting at her desk, working on a breaking news story, when the screen suddenly went blank. All the words had disappeared, and no matter how she tried, she could not retrieve the story. Her desk began melting, and her laptop sank in along with it. As she frantically tried to hold on to it, Darren walked over to her cubicle, the fury burning in his eyes. "Where's the story, Kim? We're already 15 minutes behind everyone else."

"My desk is melting, Darren!"

"I don't care, I need the story now, Kim."

That was when the sound of her phone vibrating woke her up.

She blinked groggily. It took a few seconds for her mind to adjust to consciousness and to recall where she was. Kim glanced at her watch: 4.45pm. She had been sleeping all day since making the police report in the morning, and handing over the letter, photos and hell notes – but not before taking several photos of the items, just in case. The whole incident might result in another byline for her, if the police decided to charge Johnson Lee.

Kim lay in bed staring at the ceiling as she absentmindedly reached for her phone. There were several missed calls from an unfamiliar number. She put the phone aside. Whoever was calling could wait. Kim had been having sleepless nights again. Besides the pressures of work, her mother was still sick. She had been struggling with long COVID for months, but there wasn't much that the doctors had been able to do besides prescribe bed rest and subject her to endless tests and advise her to mask up wherever she went.

Kim lived in a flat rented with two other friends, but she checked in on her mother every other day. Her mother wasn't bedridden, but she was easily tired out and needed the aid of the domestic helper with cooking and cleaning. Now Kim was contemplating a move back home, but the prospect of her mother nagging her endlessly about not being married quickly put paid to any possibility of going back.

Of late, Kim had been assessing her career. Her last promotion was more than two years ago, and her salary had only seen tiny increments since. Once upon a time, she had earned plaudits for breaking exclusives and inducing elusive newsmakers to speak. Now, five years into the job, Kim asked herself if she wanted to stay in journalism at all. The pay was poor, the hours were long and she remained low in the food chain. The choicest assignments still went to the editors' pets, especially the ones who knew when to simper and what to say and who to butter up, both in and out of the newsroom.

Worst of all, the scoops had only been rewarded with more work, usually of the painful variety. The supes apparently thought that the way to motivate reporters was to send more arrows their way, and their complaints were often dismissed with a refrain of "You need to toughen up, this is the job." It was difficult to feel that way when you were expected to do things like hang out at a hawker centre all day and ask customers why they weren't returning their plates and cutlery.

The constant snide remarks directed at the paper's journalists, both online and in person, didn't help either. At an event for a documentary about dissidents who had been jailed by the government, a fiery activist stood up and loudly denounced the newspaper for its biased reporting, before pointing a finger at Kim and proclaiming to cheers,

"*National Times*, stop this shit!" She rolled her eyes, while a friend from a foreign media outlet chuckled and said, "Yeah Kim, stop this shit hor."

Kim did still have one thing in common with other journalists: the thrill of the chase. Getting the tip-off from a reliable source, putting in the legwork to verify the information, placing all your facts and figures and quotes in a coherent narrative, and being the first to break the story. There were few things that could match the pride of seeing your byline on a story that actually mattered. But even pride could only go so far.

Just the other day, a comms person from an MNC whom she knew slightly had sent her a message on LinkedIn, asking if Kim might be interested in a role with their content team. While she found the prospect of doing public relations to be hive-inducing, it was the line "you will find the compensation generous" that caught her eye. Kim thought about her mother's health and her desire to eventually buy a flat, and knew that it was time to start planning for the future. She made a mental note to reply to the LinkedIn message.

Kim's phone vibrated again. She picked it up and saw the unfamiliar number once more. Despite her better instincts, she answered it.

"Hi, is that Kimberly?"

"Yes, who is this?"

"This is Fiona, the Prime Minister's press sec."

"Oh. Hello. How are you, Fiona?"

"I'm good, Kim. Are you free to meet tomorrow? There's something we need to discuss."

Kim sat outside the office of the press secretary and smoothed down the folds of her dress, trying not to fidget. She untied her hair and tied it up yet again. She checked her emails and messages. She usually wore comfortable clothes for work, like simple blouses and pants or jeans. Dresses were reserved for ministerial events or interviews with CEOs.

She couldn't quite fathom the reason for her nervousness. Kim had met Fiona Ang many times, and the encounters had been cordial, albeit brief. She was never among the chosen coterie who were senior enough to be granted one-on-ones, or even group interviews, with the Prime Minister. And yet, Kim had been summoned, and she now recalled stories of Fiona telling reporters things like, "You all already know the Prime Minister wants the story like this, so make sure you stick to it."

The press sec reminded her of Hillary Clinton, with her megawatt smile and her preference for power suits in shades of black or white. She was a high-flyer, only in her mid-30s and already working directly with the PM. The buzz going around was that she was his blue-eyed girl, and the role of press sec was nothing more than a stepping stone to greater glories. Fiona Ang was neither a crony nor yet another unmemorable scholar rolling off the conveyor belt: with her aptitude and savvy, she was destined for the upper echelons of government. Kim had heard that her Current Estimated Potential, that barometer of one's career prospects so beloved of the civil service, was permanent secretary. Fiona was clearly on the express elevator to the top. Some were already talking about her as a potential candidate in the next election.

The door to the office opened. Fiona stepped out in a beige pant suit and comfortable heels, and her hair was neatly tied up in a bun. There was a casual confidence about her that Kim only wished she had. Why is her skin so good, she thought, as Fiona strode towards her and proffered her hand.

"Thanks for coming down, Kim. I appreciate your time." Her grip was as firm as a man's, a quality which, though she could not explain why, made Kim nervous when she saw it in a woman.

"Sure, no problem."

"Come into my office."

The press secretary's office, painted in tasteful hues of sky blue and white, was the very definition of neat and tidy, practically spartan. Arranged around her desktop were photos of Fiona with her husband and infant children in loving embraces. On the wall directly facing the desk hung commendations from different ministries, as well as photos with her boss. Closing the door, Fiona took a seat on her leather chair and beckoned Kim to the seat across from her. It didn't look quite as comfortable as Fiona's.

"How are you, Kim?"

"I'm good. Just busy with work."

"I hope you weren't too affected by what happened yesterday."

"Oh. You heard?"

"Yes, I spoke to Jake. Are you all right?"

"I'm okay. It was just a bit weird," said Kim, laughing nervously. Barely 30 seconds into the conversation and Fiona was already dropping her boss's name.

"Let me get right to the point. That's what I called you here to discuss."

"You want to talk about the hell notes?" asked Kim.

"Yes, I do. What I am about to tell you is strictly off the record."

Kim waited and said nothing. For once, she was keeping a lid on her curiosity.

"The PM has asked me to convey a request to you."

"Request?" Kim was bewildered. She had no idea what to do with her hands. She tucked her hair behind her ears, crossed her arms, clasped her hands on her lap and repeated the process all over again. Can she tell that I'm nervous, said the internal voice in her head that invariably emerged whenever her anxiety took over.

"I know you made a police report. They have been in touch with us, and PM does not want to pursue the matter any further. He feels that it's a disturbed individual who has fallen on hard times and is just venting his frustrations. He won't act on his threats." Despite her uneasiness, Kim remained studiously silent. How the PM could possibly know that Johnson Lee was harmless was certainly a matter for contention.

"Jake also agrees that it's a minor incident, not worth reporting on." There was that allusion to the editor again. "So. PM is asking that you keep the matter to yourself. He would regard it as a personal favour."

Kim digested what she had been told. "Can I count on

your discretion, Kim?" asked Fiona pointedly, with just a hint of impatience in her tone.

The wheels were turning in Kim's head. "Who is Johnson Lee to the PM?"

The poker face that Fiona Ang projected was worthy of winning a gambling championship. She didn't respond to the query.

Kim could feel herself getting her blood up. "If it's such a minor matter, why is the PM's press sec summoning a reporter to her office? Why didn't you just tell Darren or Jake to tell me?" She sensed that Fiona had already spoken to them and obtained their assent.

Fiona suppressed a laugh. "I've always found you a bright young woman, Kim." Kim wondered how the press secretary could possibly have discerned her intelligence, considering that they had spent a combined total of 30 minutes together.

"So are we agreed?" said Fiona casually. "You won't pursue this any further?"

It was at this point that the conversation took an inexorable turn. In the days to come, when she related the story to the handful of disbelieving colleagues whom she trusted, Kim would be asked again and again why she did what she did. She did not have an answer. Maybe it was down to frustration and thwarted ambition. Maybe she saw the opportunity and went for it without thinking about the consequences. Or maybe she just didn't like being strong-armed.

"In exchange for?"

"I beg your pardon?"

She couldn't quite believe the words that were coming out of her own mouth. But she soldiered on, her heart pounding away. "You are asking me to keep my mouth shut about this man. But what do I get out of it?"

The incredulity on Fiona's face alone was almost worth the enormous risk Kim was taking. "The gratitude of the Prime Minister."

"I need something more than that."

"What would you like, Kim? CDC vouchers?" There was a none-too-subtle shift in Fiona's tone. Kim was reminded of nature documentaries where the predator stalked its prey for hours on end before pouncing on the poor creature and devouring it. It felt as if she were between the jaws of a lion.

"An hour with the PM, on any topic of my choosing."

Fiona laughed out loud. "I also want to strike Toto, but it's still not going to happen."

"Then I'll just have to keep following up with the police. I agree with Jake: a threat to the PM should be taken seriously."

"And you're confident that the police will act on your report?"

"If they don't, I'll keep following up with them. And if they still do nothing, I will just have to express my concerns in public. I'll also have to ask why the PM's press sec asked me not to act on it. Surely you agree that this is a matter of public interest."

She frowned. "This meeting is strictly off the record. I told you that at the start, Kim."

"I think you're forgetting something, Fiona."

"What's that?"

"I never agreed that it was off the record."

The way she glared at Kim could have melted a frozen lake. "Do you value your job, Kim?"

She made a show of shrugging. "I don't know, Fiona. Nowadays, being a *National Times* reporter is not very prestigious. Everyone says we are sponging off the taxpayer. I also don't see people queuing up to join us."

"Are you recording this conversation, Kim?"

"No, I'm not."

"What kind of evidence do you have to back up your claims then?"

"I have photos of the hell notes and the letter, for one. The black-and-white photos too."

Fiona scoffed. "That doesn't prove you're telling the truth."

"Maybe, but it also doesn't prove that I'm lying."

Fiona had dropped all pretence of friendliness. "Have you ever thought about what it's like to be sued, Kim?"

"All the time. But I think the PM also doesn't want any more attention on Johnson Lee, whoever he is. Or on his relationship with him." She made sure to lock eyes with Fiona before she uttered her next words. "If I really lose my job, I might just go on Instagram and tell everyone why."

Fiona was glaring at Kim in a manner that reminded her of her secondary school teacher when she failed to hand in her homework. But the reporter remembered what an old-timer once told her, "The first-generation leaders would not have hesitated to jail a journalist. Today, it's a Cabinet-level decision."

Fiona's expression remained inscrutable. She had picked up a pen and was fiddling with it with both hands. "I need you to step out for a minute, Kim." She added icily, "If you don't mind lah."

Kim got up and stepped out of the office. She could just

about hear Fiona picking up the landline as she closed the door behind her. Kim exhaled noisily and covered her mouth with her hand. There was either about to be an enormous payoff, or she was finished in Singapore journalism.

Instead of sitting, she stood ramrod stiff outside the office. Kim took out her phone and pretended to fiddle with it, while straining to hear what was being discussed in the office. She could only catch snatches here and there, but the volume of Fiona's voice was steadily increasing. "Yes, PM … terribly rude … ultimatum … can't let this stand … shall talk to Jake … can't be doing this … what? … but what if … are you sure …" There was a lengthy pause. "Yes, PM … yes … I shall speak to her."

A grand total of exactly three minutes passed before the door swung open again. Kim turned around to see that the mask had cracked. The expression on Fiona's face could best be described as a combination of livid and bewildered.

"Come in, Kim. Again." Proceeding into the office, Fiona sat back down in her leather chair once more. She took in the sight of Kim, seated across from her and fiddling with her hands once again. She seemed to be sizing her up the way one might assess a cut of meat at the wet market. This went on for a full minute before she finally spoke.

"PM has acceded to your request. You get thirty minutes. You have two days to come up with questions and submit them to me. The interview will be conducted in his office on Monday morning." In a tone colder than a blast from the freezer, Fiona added, "The Prime Minister would love to entertain you today, but he actually has to run the country."

Kim felt as if she had struck Toto. "I'm not submitting anything to you. I will ask him whatever I see fit."

Fiona inhaled and exhaled noisily. "Fine. But I'm going to need you to delete whatever photos you took."

Kim reached into her tote bag and took out her phone. Scrolling through the photos, she tapped on the screen rapidly and turned it towards Fiona. She tapped the screen again and deleted the images. "A show of good faith."

"And how do I know you haven't saved the photos somewhere else?"

"You don't. But I am also trusting that I won't be blacklisted by government agencies going forward."

Fiona sneered. "You trust us to do that, Kim?"

"Of course I do. The Prime Minister is an honourable man." She couldn't resist adding, "He will even go out of his way to protect the vulnerable."

In five years of reporting, Kim had never been to the Istana before. Wearing her most formal and most expensive work dress, she entered the premises through the rear gate at Cavenagh Road that morning with the assigned videographer. Her pulse raced as the security officers on duty did the standard baggage checks and perused their press passes.

As they waited outside the PM's office, she politely declined the offers of coffee and cake from the kindly aunties in the cubicles outside. Kim pored over the questions in her notebook one more time. She had stayed up late the night before to ensure that they were just right, with as little wiggle room as possible. There were literally a hundred questions she could have asked the PM, but she decided to focus on social policies and migrant worker issues, the two issues she cared about most.

She had enjoyed watching Darren's jaw drop while informing him that she had scored an interview with the Prime Minister. He was good at his job and guided her well, but also had a tendency to adopt a wise, avuncular persona, with the attendant condescending tone. He was especially prone to this when dealing with young female reporters. The rumour was that Darren had even gone out with a few, but he had never tried it on with Kim. Which was fortunate for Darren, since she might have clawed his eyes out.

A secretary emerged from the office. "The Prime Minister will see you now."

He was sitting at a large wooden desk which was bare but for three laptops and a couple of family photos. Behind him stood a showcase filled with photos of the PM with leaders of state, alongside other bric-a-brac. Fiona stood off to the side holding a clear plastic folder, wearing a nonplussed expression. Arising to shake their hands, the PM towered over Kim and the videographer. He's even taller than on television, she thought. As the videographer busied himself with setting up the camera and the lights, as well as miking up reporter and interviewee, the PM sat serenely at his desk and eyed them astutely. "How is your mother, Kimberly?"

The question spooked Kim. "She's well, PM. She was very excited to hear that I am interviewing you." She had never seen proof of it, but the chatter in the media scene was that the Internal Security Department had a file on every single reporter. Kim half-expected the PM to ask if she had enjoyed the chicken rice with tau gey that she had eaten for dinner the night before.

"Please convey my best wishes to her. She has raised a fine young woman." Kim was tempted to ask the Prime Minister if he wanted to discuss her love life too, but decided that she had tempted fate enough.

After a brief sound check, the videographer was done. He nodded at Kim and the PM. "We're rolling now."

"So. What would you like to ask me?" asked the Prime Minister.

Kim had gotten this far on sheer guts, at great risk to herself. Now she was on the verge of the biggest scoop of her career. But she would not be able to live with herself if she didn't at least pose the query.

"Who is Johnson Lee, and what is your relationship to him?"

The expression on Fiona's face suggested that she would like to have Kim arrested on the spot. As for the Prime Minister, there was a twinkle in his eye. "You can ask me anything at all, Kimberly. Except that."

Kim's eyes darted everywhere except to the Prime Minister's face. Had she already made a fatal error? That was when she spotted the black-and-white photo in the showcase behind him.

It was of a young man standing before a roadside stall, beaming at the camera as he held a little boy in his arms. The boy, sucking on a lollipop, looked back at the camera curiously. Was he thinking about the day, decades in the future, when he might have to face questions from an equally curious journalist about the young man and what he meant to him?

The courageous, or perhaps foolhardy, reporter caught the Prime Minister's gaze. His canny grin gave nothing away.

The newsroom was abuzz that evening with chatter over Kim's scoop, which was pushed out in record time. The editors had decided to split the story into several parts for maximum mileage, and the first part had already gotten a thousand shares in the first hour.

The PM had been as good as his word. He had well-rehearsed talking points for the evergreen red button issues and dodged the queries he didn't want to address, but still came up with great quotes. He even gave her a full hour, over the protestations of Fiona. Combined with quotes from analysts, comprehensive facts and figures, and the viewpoints of those affected by the policies in question, it all added up to a fairly weighty story.

Kim sat at her desk, exhausted but satisfied. It had been a long time since she had felt good about the job.

"Well done, Kimberly." She turned to her left to find Jake, proffering his hand. Kim took it and responded with an equally firm grip.

"How did you manage to land the interview?"

Kim observed Jake carefully. Had Fiona or the PMO not told him what transpired? She couldn't tell.

She contemplated the question at length before answering.

"Because I'm a good reporter."

The Woodcutter

Long ago, when tigers used to smoke, there lived a young woodcutter in Cheonan. He came from a poor family and had little in the way of material possessions. But he was happy, for he had a beautiful wife who loved him, and children who adored him, and he earned an honest living. He was a pious man too, making offerings to his ancestors daily and worshipping at the altar of Haneullim, the Lord of Heaven. "Bless me, ancestors," he intoned daily. "Never let me dishonour my father and mother. Let my children grow to become good women who will find good husbands."

The woodcutter lived a quiet life, providing for his family and living in harmony with his fellow villagers. Because he was a virtuous man, the gods favoured him and his family and gave them plenty to eat. And even though there was talk of murderous invaders pillaging the land, the village carried on with everyday life. After all, the harvest was coming, and there was nothing to reap if you did not sow.

And then the dokkaebi came for him.

As a child, the woodcutter had been told that the short, stumpy goblins were a mischievous lot. They were said to be *nature deities, or spirits that possessed inanimate objects. They were easily angered but essentially harmless. If you earned the favour of the dokkaebi, they would grant you gifts of silver and gold with their magical clubs, which could manifest anything you desired. If you incurred their wrath, they might play cruel tricks on you, such as elongating your nose.*

But these goblins were different. They were called the gae dokkaebi, and they fed off the suffering of others. Time and again, they overran the land, leaving pain and misery in their wake. They were a hideous lot too, with red faces and sharp, spiky horns that would cut you if you touched them. And the gae dokkaebi spoke a maddeningly familiar, yet utterly unknown language, gibbering away like monkeys.

The gae dokkaebi came to the woodcutter's village one night in a burst of sound and fury, setting fire to several houses and terrifying everyone. They rounded up all the young men and threatened to kill the women and children if they did not cooperate. They took the men from their families to a faraway land that he did not know. Down they went into the depths of a coal mine, right into the heart of a mountain.

Day and night, the woodcutter and the other men, who came from different villages all over Korea, were forced to harvest coal for the goblins. This was sold to the inhabitants of nearby villages, and the dokkaebi kept the profits. They were cruel masters, urging the men on with horsehide whips and depriving them of food when they did not produce enough coal. The dokkaebi would also keep them in line by threatening to return to their respective villages and seize the women, who would be used for even more sinister purposes.

Since they did not speak a common language, the men were largely reduced to communicating with the dokkaebi via gestures. Their meals were awful too: they were fed once a day, with some rice, half a bowl of soup whose flavour was odd to them, two strips of pickled radish and some fermented black soybeans. To amuse themselves, the dokkaebi would beat one of the men with their clubs every so often. They regularly went too far, leaving the man bloodied and unconscious when they were done. At other times, they would take their tools away and make them dig for coal with their bare hands. The woodcutter was often beaten too, but he would not give the goblins the satisfaction of crying out in pain. Instead, he stared into the distance and took the beating without uttering a word.

The woodcutter's hands, along with his heart, became hard and callused, and his frame gaunt and wiry. Some of the men dropped dead while others simply gave up: they laid down and would not work anymore. These were taken away by the goblins and never seen again. Among the men, there was talk of the bodies being used in magic rituals, and reanimated corpses that roamed the nearby woods. For no one really knew what the goblins did when they retreated into the common hanok they shared, though the din of raucous feasting and drinking constantly emanated from within. Occasionally, one could hear screams.

But even in the darkness of the mine, there was still light. For whenever he was able to rest, the woodcutter shut his eyes and thought about the family he had left behind in Cheonan. He would never forget the tears of his children, nor the anguish in his wife's eyes, and her parting words as the dokkaebi took him away.

"Yeobo, jebal dol-a wajwo."

Darling, please come back to me.

The Woodcutter

It was on the narrow step outside Tanjong Pagar MRT station, just beyond the verdant sidewalk that she had passed a thousand times before, that Seo-yoon tripped and fell. She winced and clutched her right knee, where a bruise was already beginning to form. Was it down to one too many glasses of soju? Seo-yoon didn't know. But it felt as if someone had turned a switch, or snapped their fingers and uttered an incantation.

On her way home, Seo-yoon found herself thinking of Harabeoji and the day in her childhood when she tripped and injured the very same knee while playing in the park. Her grandfather had gently picked her up and carried her home, as she bawled into his shoulder. Seo-yoon could still conjure up the smell of his sweat on his furrowed brow, and how big and strong he was, and the way the tattoo of a majestic white tiger on his bicep peeked out from beneath his shirt sleeve. She only ever saw it on sweltering days when Harabeoji took his shirt off. It was highly unusual to see body art among the older generation, since tattoos were associated with gangs. Once, when she asked why he had it, all Harabeoji would say was, "To give thanks."

She knew what Harabeoji would say if he saw her. You must have been whistling at night again, he would say in the gruff, gravelly Korean Seo-yoon had heard all her life. You will summon the dokkaebi without even knowing it. Long after Seo-yoon's mother had married a Singaporean and moved the whole family to the city-state, he would invoke the old country and its beliefs.

Harabeoji rarely had much to say. It was only when Seo-yoon, his favourite grandchild, slid into his lap and begged for a story that he would relent with a tale or two. Later that night, as she lay in bed nursing her knee, she thought about the story her grandfather had told her time and again.

"Once upon a time, there lived a handsome young woodcutter in the shadow of the Diamond Mountains. He longed for love, but could not afford to marry."

"And the deer told him how to marry a beautiful girl!"

"Hey, who's telling the story here?"

"Joesonghabnida, Harabeoji," apologised Seo-yoon. "Please continue."

The old man smiled indulgently. "One day, the woodcutter came upon a stricken deer which was being pursued by a hunter. And because he was a kind-hearted man who would not even harm a fly, he helped the deer get away. In return, the deer, who was a servant of the mountain god Sansin, told him how to fulfil his greatest wish."

"Why is it that the deer can talk," said Seo-yoon, repeating the question she asked each time the story was told.

"Because magic was still possible, Seo-yoon-ah. Today, it has been all but forgotten."

"So what did the deer say to the woodcutter, Harabeoji?"

"It said, 'At the next full moon, go to the lake at the top of the mountain, where the fairies from heaven come to bathe. Take the clothes of one of them, for without them, she would not be able to return to heaven. That is when you can take her as your wife.'"

"Is that how you met Halmeoni?"

Harabeoji turned to his wife. He grinned. "Yes, that's

exactly how we met. She came down from heaven, and I married her."

Harabeoji never talked about himself or the past. Even as a child, Seo-yoon could tell that there was much he kept to himself. She saw it in the way he sat by himself, contemplating endlessly, smoking one cigarette after another. She could see it too in the pained, desperate way he gazed upon Halmeoni. Was Seo-yoon the only one who could see it? She didn't know, because she didn't dare ask any of her relatives. She realised that she hardly knew anything about her grandfather, other than the fact that he came from Cheonan in South Chungcheong province, and had lived through terrible times.

"Omma," said a teenaged Seo-yoon to her mother as she was cooking dinner one day. "Why is Harabeoji always so quiet?"

"Because he has suffered a lot," said Seo-yoon's mother as she prepared the banchan, a dazzling array of red and green and yellow side dishes to be spread out on the dining table on small plates. Like her father, the youngest of seven girls did not say very much. Perhaps it was a family trait. It seemed to Seo-yoon that words were a valuable currency, to be carefully spent only on special occasions.

"How?"

Seo-yoon's mother remained focused on her chores. But what she said next stunned her daughter. "The Japanese took him away in 1942 and forced him to work in a coal mine. He was only 20. They kept him in Japan for three years."

"What?"

"When he finally came home, he, your grandmother and your aunties had to live through the 6.25 War too. It was a miracle that they didn't die."

"Why didn't you tell me this before?"

"There was no need to." Seo-yoon's mother halted her tasks. She only made eye contact when she had something important to say. "You must treasure your grandfather, Seo-yoon. You will never know what he went through." She went back to preparing dinner and did not speak of it again.

In the years that followed, it became a topic that was only mentioned in hushed tones between Seo-yoon and her cousins at family gatherings in Seoul and in Singapore. All were born in the 1980s or later, while Seo-yoon lived nearly all her life in Singapore. None of them knew very much about the Second World War or how it had affected Korea, nor did they particularly care. But Seo-yoon did some googling and came away horrified. One source said that between 1939 and 1945, hundreds of thousands of Koreans were taken from their country and forced to labour in Japan. Many of them never made it home.

It made Seo-yoon shiver to think about what the Japanese might have done to her grandfather. How had Harabeoji survived all by himself, with no friends or relatives to count on? It was a miracle that he wasn't buried in an unmarked grave in some remote part of Japan or shipped back as ashes in a box, as so many others were. And though she asked her mother and aunts and uncles many times, none of them truly knew how their father had managed to come home.

One afternoon, while she was at her grandparents' flat, Seo-yoon plucked up the courage to speak to her grandmother. That was when she knew never to ask again.

"Halmeoni?"

"Yes, Seo-yoon-ah," she said brightly, her knitting needles clicking away.

"What was it like when they took Harabeoji to Japan?"

Her grandmother's reaction stuck a knife in Seo-yoon's heart. She put her knitting needles down and sighed. She seemed to deflate, like a balloon that had run out of helium.

"Halmeoni?" But the old woman turned away and would not look at her granddaughter. Almost in slow motion, her body was wracked with sobs. It was the only time Seo-yoon ever saw her cry.

Seo-yoon was crying too. Though she had never done it before as an adult, she held her grandmother tight.

"I was terrified that I would never see him again," said Halmeoni, her voice breaking. "I will never forgive them for what they did."

One evening, as the woodcutter sat outside the entrance to the mine, nursing his bruised hands, a white tiger came by. Now, you might wonder why he did not flee in fear at once, or why the big cat did not pounce on him and devour him. But this was in the old days when plants and animals talked, and the noble tigers still roamed the land. The woodcutter got up and bowed deeply, for the wise white tiger was revered.

"How are you today, seonsaengnim?"

"I am well," said the tiger, propping himself before the woodcutter, puffing away on his pipe. He had a stern expression, but his manner was gentle and his tone kind. His eyes were of the brightest blue, and his stripes lent him a regal air that no other creature in the forest had. "And how are you?"

"I am far from home and from my family. The dokkaebi took me here and forced me to labour for them."

The tiger bristled, his whiskers seeming to glow in the moonlight. "When was the last time you saw your family?"

"I do not know, seonsaengnim. I fear that a day will come when I cannot recall the faces of my wife and children."

The clouds of smoke obscured the tiger's face as he puffed away. "Do you miss them?"

"With all my heart."

"What would you give to see them again?"

"Everything. Anything."

The tiger's face was inscrutable in the dark. "Hear me now," proclaimed the feline as he stood up to his full height. In the light of the full moon, the majesty of the white tiger could be seen in his full glory, his powerful limbs glistening. "Your plight has not gone unnoticed by the gods, nor have the vile deeds of the gae dokkaebi. Sansin has been watching, and he has sent me to you."

The woodcutter fell to his knees. "What must I do, seonsaengnim?"

"The magic of the dokkaebi is powerful, but their weakness is for buckwheat jelly." With that, a large plate piled high with the delicious treat appeared before the woodcutter. "Take this to their hanok and leave it at the door, that they may feast upon it. As they sleep off their meal tonight, go into the *house. There you will find a bangmangi, the magic club of the dokkaebi. When you thump it and say the right words, it will give you whatever you want. Take it, for it is your just reward for all that you have suffered."*

The tiger seemed to blend into the stillness of the night. "Once you have secured the bangmangi, come back here, and I will take you away from this accursed place."

The woodcutter did as he was told. Hidden outside their hanok, he could hear the dokkaebi cackling loudly as they feasted. This eventually gave way to loud snores as they fell asleep. Soon, the lights in the house went out, and the woodcutter made his move. Stealing into the hanok, he felt his way along in the dark, tiptoeing around the snoring goblins, and soon located it: the rough-hewn club of the dokkaebi, as long as a man's forearm, that they carried as they barked orders at the labourers every day. The woodcutter exited the house and closed the door as gently as he could. When he turned around, one of them was waiting for him.

The dokkaebi leered at the woodcutter in the moonlight. It was the ugliest visage he had ever seen, all red and twisted, its fangs pointy and bared. The goblin would surely raise the alarm at any moment. But something came over the woodcutter. He raised the bangmangi and hit the goblin on the head with all his might. The dokkaebi fell to the ground unconscious.

But the woodcutter did not stop there, for he raised the club again and again, until his face was bathed in a crimson shower, and the goblin was more pulp than flesh, and it was no longer a part of the living. When the woodcutter was done, he was panting and gasping for air. He wiped the club on the goblin's hanbok, and spat in its face.

As he prepared to leave, the woodcutter took in the common fire outside the hanok that burned night and day. In the bitter cold of winter, it was where dokkaebi and men alike warmed themselves whenever they could. He turned back towards the hanok again. He picked up a few heavy rocks that were nearby and piled them at the entrance to the house, preventing the door from opening. Then he picked up the burning logs from the fire and placed them all around the hanok. He backed away and waited.

The wooden house caught fire in no time. That was when the dokkaebi awoke, and the frantic banging at the door could be heard. Squealing away in their accursed language, the goblins screamed and cursed and cried for help. But the woodcutter did not move a muscle. The fire crackled away, consuming the hanok and everything that was in it. He made sure to wait till the screams faded into the dark before leaving.

The woodcutter made his way back to the entrance of the mine, where the white tiger was waiting. The big cat looked him up and down. He did not comment on the blood on his face and hands, nor on the blaze in the distance. Instead, he beckoned to the woodcutter.

"Get on me. It is time to go."

A few weeks after Seo-yoon's fall, there came terrible news: Harabeoji suffered a massive stroke. Halmeoni had come home from the market early that day, to find her husband on the ground, confused and incoherent. She called Seo-yoon's mother in a panic. The paramedics got him to the hospital in time, but the left side of his body was now paralysed, and he couldn't speak.

It was decided that he and Halmeoni would come and live with Seo-yoon and her mother. Her father had long passed and she was an only child, so it was down to mother and daughter to help care for the stricken old man. A thorough renovation of their flat was undertaken in order to accommodate the ramps and his wheelchair. Bars were installed in the toilets and handrails in the spare room, as well as a seat in the shower. A helper was also hired, and after the initial period of adjustment, the family gradually settled into the role of caregivers.

Harabeoji needed help with everything: eating, brushing his teeth, going to the washroom, showering. Halmeoni would have struggled just to lift him off the toilet bowl by herself, let alone getting him into bed. And yet, she patiently waited upon him, waving the helper away and making sure to take on the most intimate tasks. Because he was left-handed and could no longer use his dominant hand, she brushed his teeth morning and night, gently and methodically. She changed his diapers whenever he could not make it to the toilet in time. She even fed him like a toddler, cutting up his food into pieces so he would not choke, and wiping the drool off his cheek. The sight of this made Seo-yoon's heart ache, but it left her in awe to see the love of her grandmother for her husband.

And yet, the agony in his eyes never went away. She knew that she could never ask her grandfather, but Seo-yoon pondered the question time and again: what burdens from the war was Harabeoji still carrying?

With the bangmani strapped to his back, the woodcutter rode the tiger for what felt like thousands of ri. On and on they went, down the mountain and past lakes and rivers and fields. Eventually, they came to a village in a lush green valley, where the tiger beckoned for him to get off.

As he dismounted, the wise old tiger fixed his blue orbs on the woodcutter. "This is where I must leave you."

"Where am I, seonsaengnim?"

"You are in a place of peace and plenty. The dokkaebi will never find you here."

The woodcutter was crestfallen. "But where is home?"

"That is what you must decide for yourself."

"Please, seonsaengnim. Won't you take me home?"

"The dokkaebi have defiled this land and its people. They deserve no mercy." The wise old eyes of the tiger remained still as he spoke. "But it was not up to you to decide their fate."

The woodcutter was crestfallen, but a fury arose in him. "I hope I burned every last one of them," he said defiantly.

"And that is why I can bring you no further," said the tiger. "I wish you good fortune. Perhaps we shall meet again." The woodcutter bowed deeply to the big cat. When he straightened up, he had gone.

Behind the woodcutter, curious villagers had already gathered. They murmured and pointed at the interloper in their midst, wary about his intentions. One of them was a lithe young woman with eyes like a cat. The woodcutter could not help but notice her delicate features, and the fairness of her skin. She smiled at him, and he smiled back.

Time passed. Harabeoji gradually got better, though he could not function without his wheelchair or the women of the house. His words were slurred and it took an effort to understand him, but he seemed to be in good spirits. A physiotherapist was hired, who would come by several times a week with her equipment to put the old man through rehabilitation exercises. The helper and Seo-yoon took it in turns to help lift him out of the wheelchair and put him in position. Harabeoji never lost his temper and did whatever was asked of him. In time, he could move his left arm and hand again, and even cross his legs. But they could all see the frustration in his eyes.

Every morning, with Seo-yoon's aid, the helper would lift Harabeoji into his wheelchair and wheel him to the window in the living room, where he would soak in a bit of sunshine and watch the world go by. In the evenings, she wheeled him downstairs and placed him at the nearby park, while she chatted with the other helpers. It was a lonely existence for the old man, since there were few Koreans in their estate and he spoke only a smattering of English. Seo-yoon's relatives came by whenever they could, but everyone had work commitments and their own families to tend to.

Seo-yoon helped improvise a rig on the wheelchair, where she placed a tablet so he could watch Korean dramas. With enough practice, he became proficient at navigating the different channels and streaming services. Seo-yoon would sit with him while doing her work, so that he would not be on his own. She held his hand as if she were a child again. His grip, even on his weaker right hand, was as firm as ever.

One day, Seo-yoon sat next to her grandfather, reading a book, when he reached for her hand and squeezed it. She turned her head up to see a lopsided grin on his face. He was still slurring, but his words were crystal clear to her. "Read me a story, Seo-yoon-ah."

She couldn't help shedding a tear and beaming at the same time. She picked up the washcloth, an ever-present on the wheelchair handles, and wiped the drool from his mouth, which now ran in a meandering stream rather than a constant river. Then she ran to her room and grabbed a book with dog-eared pages that her parents had given her as a child. She already knew the story by heart, but felt the need to do it the proper way. Sitting before Harabeoji, she flipped through the pages and cleared her throat. As the first words came out of her mouth, the old man's eyes lit up.

"On a day in the distant past, there lived a woodcutter in the shadow of the Diamond Mountains. He longed for love, but could not afford to marry."

The woodcutter paused his work for a breather. Dusk was near.

He had been tilling the fields all day, and it was backbreaking work. But he didn't mind, for it meant that there was food on the table, and a bulwark against the coming winter.

It had taken him some time to earn the trust of the villagers, being the stranger who appeared from nowhere with an incredible tale to tell. He learned how to be a farmer, and worked hard to become good at it, eventually fitting into the rhythms of the village. But he never told anyone about the bangmangi, which he used to conjure up food or money whenever there wasn't enough. He carefully hid it in the roof of the hanok he was given to live in, and only ever used it sparingly.

"Greetings, nongbu." *The woodcutter froze. He had not heard that voice in a full year now.*

"Good evening, seonsaengnim," *he said, turning around and bowing deeply to the teacher. The white tiger reclined at the edge of the fields, smoking his pipe.* "How are you this day?"

"I am well. I see that you are now a farmer."

"Yes. I learned over many months."

"And you have made a good life for yourself," *said the tiger.*

The woodcutter turned his head behind him toward the house, not too far away, that he shared with the woman with the cat-like eyes. She was tending to the garden. She caught his eye and waved, smiling as she cradled the bump on her stomach. He beamed and waved back, casting a nervous backwards glance at the tiger as he did so.

"Do not worry. You are the only one who can see me."

"Why have you returned, seonsaengnim? Was it not enough that you left me here to fend for myself?" *said the woodcutter bitterly.*

"The dokkaebi have been driven from your village. Your wife and children are safe." *The woodcutter was speechless. He had not thought of his family in a long time.*

The tiger exhaled, the smoke clouds from his pipe filling the air. "Are you ready to go home now?"

He looked over again at the woman who was now his

wife. He reminisced about the days they had spent tilling the fields together and the nights they had shared in each other's arms. He remembered how she had vouched for him with the other villagers when they did not trust him, and the way she showed him the love and kindness that he had not known for so very long.

But he also remembered his wife's desperate eyes the day he was taken away, and the tears of his children.

"Please take me home, seonsaengnim."

Of late, Harabeoji had taken to awaking in the middle of the night, shouting and crying. At the beginning, Seo-yoon would sprint to her grandparents' room, where the old man whimpered as his wife comforted him. He would mumble incomprehensibly in Korean, before calming down and eventually falling back to sleep, exhausted. This happened on many nights.

One night, Seo-yoon was awoken again by the familiar racket of shouting and thrashing. She knew that there was no real need to do so, but she still dragged herself out of bed. Seo-yoon proceeded groggily to her grandparents' room, where the door remained closed. Putting her ear to the door to check that everything was okay, she heard a phrase, faintly uttered but still clear as day, "Watashi ga kanojo to wakareta toki, kanojo wa ninshin shite ita."

This puzzled Seo-yoon. She recognised Harabeoji's voice, but he had spoken in Japanese. Carefully making her way back to her room, Seo-yoon repeated the words to herself.

She picked up her phone and tapped out a note, spelling it as best as she could in English. Tossing it aside, she went back to sleep, promptly forgetting all about it when she awoke.

It was weeks later, while having dinner with a Japanese friend, that Seo-yoon suddenly recalled the incident. She took out her phone and showed the note to him, who spoke it out loud and looked puzzled.

"Have you been watching some Japanese mystery series or something?" asked the friend, arching an eyebrow.

"No," Seo-yoon said, intrigued. "I just heard it somewhere and wanted to know what it means."

"It means 'she was pregnant when I left her'."

When the woodcutter opened his eyes again, it was spring, and he was at the entrance to his village. Once more, the tiger had taken him across multitudes of ri, with the bangmangi strapped to his back. They had left in the dead of night, without so much as a farewell to the woman with the cat-like eyes. He feared that if he tried to explain himself to her, he would not be able to leave.

Once again, he dismounted the tiger. But the woodcutter could not bring himself to enter the village. Though he did not expect an answer, he asked the question anyway. "What do I do now, seonsaengnim?"

"Love your wife. Provide for your children. Live a good life. You deserve it."

"But what about ..."

"You will never see her again."

The woodcutter broke down. "Why was I allowed to be with her?"

"No one knows the ways of Haneullim. He sifts us like wheat, that the chaff may be disposed of, and our fates are not our own."

"It's not fair."

"Indeed. It is not."

"I can't live like this."

The wise old eyes of the white tiger gazed upon the woodcutter. "You can. You must." The woodcutter wiped his tears away and bowed deeply, arising to find that the tiger had left him by himself once more.

"Yeobo! Yeobo!" His wife ran to him, yelling frantically. She melted into his arms, weeping tears of joy. "You're home. You're home."

The woodcutter was crying too. "I am so sorry, yeobo. I will never leave you again."

Mother and daughter were in the kitchen once more, making dinner. Preparing meals now took twice as long, given that they were cooking for five, while Harabeoji required a soft diet so that he wouldn't choke. The banchan remained a must. Seo-yoon's mother didn't trust the helper with the cooking, so mother and daughter became an inseparable unit in the kitchen.

A thought came to Seo-yoon's mind, like a bolt from the blue. Could it really be?

"Omma," said Seo-yoon. "What year were you born?"

"1950, just before the war. Why?"

"And when was Sixth Aunt born?"

"1941. Why do you want to know?"

The wheels were turning in Seo-yoon's mind. Halmeoni did not give birth while Harabeoji was in Japan. Her mother was only born after World War II. Her grandfather was all alone in Japan, fighting to survive. He had to fend for himself.

Or did he?

"Omma," said Seo-yoon tentatively. "Do I have another uncle or auntie in Japan?"

Her mother put down the tongs. Whenever she made eye contact with Seo-yoon, it felt as if there were no secrets between them. "Your grandfather is only human, Seo-yoon," she said firmly, in a tone that her daughter had not heard before. "Humans make mistakes, especially when they are afraid and have no one else to count on."

It was the way she said it that made Seo-yoon sure. "Even your grandfather."

Not even a dokkaebi, or a white tiger for that matter, could have interrupted the tense silence that followed. For the past was a faraway land that no one could reach, and all that mattered was ensuring that dinner was served on time.

The Chicken Task Force

In the bowels of the Ministry building, Associate Professor Edward Low sat in the canteen with his old friend Steven Goh, nursing their customary kopi. A decade after they both joined the civil service on the same day, it remained their weekly ritual. But Edward was not in his usual chatty mood that day.

Steven asked the question that had been on Edward's mind for days on end. "How come you kena and not Harry? He's senior to you, right?"

"Cos of his surname."

"What?"

"Minister said we shouldn't have a man named Harry Kuey in charge of the task force. Optics very bad."

"A man named Harry Kuey …. oh, I get it now," said Steven, bursting into peals of laughter.

"I'm glad you find this so funny. Really."

"Sorry lah. But you have to admit it's funny what: a literal hairy chicken in charge of the Chicken Task Force."

"It's not going to be funny when you see my face all over social media as chair of this … task force."

The two men were scientists who had started out in academia before joining the government, as they wanted to work on public policy to improve the lives of Singaporeans in little ways. Family men who expected regular working hours and quiet, unspectacular careers, neither had anticipated the sudden nature of unpleasant arrows that came flying at them out of the blue.

"Did you try asking if they could change the name?"

Edward sighed. "I did. But the PS likes it. He thinks CTF has a nice ring to it. Better than the original name."

"What was the original name?"

"Task Force on Controlling Chicken Population. The TFOCCP."

"Ha! Who came up with CTF anyway?"

"Must be some scholar. And now I have to be the public face of it."

"When is the presser?"

"Monday."

"Well. I don't think there will be that many reporters, right?"

"I don't know. I just don't want to be a meme."

"It will be fine lah, Ed. Just be as boring as possible. The story will die down by the next news cycle."

"Do you know what PS said?"

"What?"

"He might be retiring soon."

"Really?"

"Yes, he's looking for a successor. He strongly hinted that it's between me and James, depending on how well we run this task force."

"What? Seriously?"

"Yes, really."

"What is this, Perm Sec Audition Task Force?"

"Why is there even a need for this task force?" asked Edward, his voice rising several decibels, attracting turned heads from nearby tables. Forcing his volume down a few notches, he whispered, "Why can't the residents and the Agency just handle this on their own?"

"Everybody is so woke now mah," said Steven, rolling his eyes as he sipped his coffee. "Chickens also must protect. Plus gahmen must show how much they love to consult people."

"They do, huh," said Edward drily.

"Yes, they do it right before ignoring them."

"I have to meet these CTF people every week loh. The animal welfare groups are the worst, I tell you. Really damn one kind."

"Why, what do they do?"

"It's that woman," said Edward, "the one with the auntie glasses and the shrill voice. And oh my God, that pompous tone. She threatened to take it to social media if we even discussed the possibility of culling chickens."

"So, the usual lah."

"You should have seen Pat's face. I thought he was going to have a stroke."

"Pat is old school lah. He's too used to people kowtowing to the gahmen. So what did you say?"

"What else could I say? I told her that culling is only a last resort."

"That's nice."

"And now I have to go and brief reporters. Wah lau."

"Just remember: don't get paggro when you get a question you don't want to answer. You're not a minister, so you can't afford to offend the MSM. Make sure you smile too."

"Is this a press con or a modelling assignment?"

"It's both, Ed. You should know that by now."

Amid the glare of the camera lights in the cavernous conference room, Edward sat at the rectangular oak table and shuffled the notes before him for the 20th time. Besides the wireless conference mics and place cards for the panellists, there was a spread of smartphones and digital recorders around them, as if someone was playing a particularly messy game of cards with the devices as chips. He had counted more than a dozen reporters and cameramen in attendance, seated in neat rows of black plastic chairs with writing pads.

Edward turned to his right. His co-chair Patrick Lim was a rotund, middle-aged man at the tail end of a long career in the civil service. The idealism and passion had been bled out of him inch by inch over the years, like the juices from a slow-roasted fowl.

Just an hour before, Pat had insisted that Edward chair the event by himself, speaking so vociferously that one would have thought he was about to burst a blood vessel. It was only when the permanent secretary said, "We need to present a united front, Pat," in a tone that suggested he would have happily sent Pat to the slaughterhouse to be eviscerated, that he quietened down and did as he was told.

To Edward's left was his other co-chair, Associate Professor James Ong. In a decade in the civil service, Edward could not recall meeting a more nakedly ambitious man. He was barely 40, young for a tenured academic. Edward wasn't that much older than him, but James, with his still boyish features and trim physique, was a spring chicken compared to all of them. He reminded Edward of Sean Connery's line from *The Hunt for Red October*, "There is little room in Tupolev's heart for anyone but Tupolev."

The young woman from the communications ministry checked their mics and place cards for the last time. Edward recalled a story he had once heard about her calling up a journalist in a huff and yelling, "You have misquoted our director and damaged the country!" After that, he had taken to calling her Bambi – in his mind, of course.

"Ready when you are, Prof Low," she whispered.

He cleared his throat. "Thank you all for coming. Welcome to the first media briefing," said Edward, drawing in a sharp intake of breath before he uttered the dreaded words, "of the Chicken Task Force." He cast his gaze across the room and saw only poker faces among the reporters, who clutched copies of his statement and had their hands poised above their keyboards.

"I am Associate Professor Edward Low. I'm a Deputy Secretary for the Agency and also co-chair of the CTF. With me today are my fellow co-chairs: Director of Poultry Services Patrick Lim and the CTF's scientific advisor, Assistant Professor James Ong, who is also my fellow Deputy Secretary. We have called this press conference to inform you of the measures we have taken to control the wild chicken population in New Town."

The whir of camera shutters filled the air as Edward spoke. He paused to inhale deeply. Years ago, Edward had undergone a course conducted by a media trainer, engaged by the Ministry to instruct all senior officials facing the media. The two most important takeaways: slow down and enunciate your words clearly, and remember to breathe and take regular pauses.

"There have been multiple complaints from the residents of New Town about an excess of wild chickens in the area. Over the past few months, this has led to many issues such as fowl spilling onto the roads and blocking traffic, and waking residents in the early morning with their crowing." Edward thought back to the lengthy arguments he had had with the staffers who drafted his speech. Instead of using terms such as "free-roaming" and "disamenities", he had insisted that the statement be written in plain language. Edward sometimes wondered if these staffers, with their shiny degrees and social media accounts, had ever learned English.

"The Agency aims to address this issue comprehensively. However, we are conscious of the New Town residents' concerns about protecting wildlife. A Chicken Task Force has therefore been formed, comprising residents, officials from the Ministry and the Agency, representatives from animal welfare groups and the Town Council. Its goal is to bring down the population of wild chickens, which currently numbers around 300, by half within the next three months."

Edward cleared his throat and went on to the next page. "Some of the measures we have rolled out include educating residents not to feed the chickens, trimming the grass in areas near homes to prevent them from nesting and placing nets on trees so that they do not roost there. We have also relocated some of the chickens to farms, and organised egg hunts for residents.

"In addition, we have been giving the chickens Ovistop, a contraceptive feed. All of these measures have been ongoing for two weeks, and we will give an update on them in another fortnight. We feel confident that the target of reducing the poultry population by fifty per cent will be met within our time frame. Once this is achieved, we will ease off on our measures, and also monitor the situation to ensure that the wild chicken population remains at a manageable level."

Edward paused once more. He already knew what he would see if he turned to his left or right: Pat, timorous and miserable, and James fiddling with his wedding band as he stared straight ahead. He braced himself. "We will now take your questions."

Hands shot up all across the room. Edward knew it was too much to hope that there would not be any queries. It seemed appropriate that he was bathed in the glare of the camera lights, since it all felt like one long, pointless performance. It also meant he could barely make out the faces before him. Edward pointed at one at random.

"Good afternoon, Prof Low. Kimberly Neo from *The National Times*." She spoke with confidence and sounded well-informed. It was the kind of reporter Edward hated the most. "Could you please explain the reasoning behind the formation of this task force, and why there was a need to get residents and animal activists involved in the process, given that chickens are not a protected species?"

"Thank you for the question, Kimberly. The Ministry and the Agency felt it was important to be proactive and to take a consultative approach to this matter. We want to be as open and transparent about our policies as possible." Except where it might cost the government votes, thought Edward. It was a softball opener, easily deflected, but he knew that it was a common tactic used by journalists to soften up newsmakers before pitching the harder questions.

"This seems like a minor matter as compared to more pressing national issues like say, inflation or housing prices. While I understand that getting feedback from stakeholders is important, wouldn't it have been easier to do that first, before letting the Environment Agency take the lead?"

I also think so loh, thought Edward. "I realise it may seem like chicken feed to some – if you will excuse the pun – but this is an ongoing issue." He paused to take in the one or two polite guffaws at his little joke, which the trainer said always helped to disarm the audience and make you appear more likeable.

"There are some 10,000 residents in New Town, which is one of the smallest wards, and their quality of life has been significantly impacted. We also have to consider that wild chickens can lay between 250 and 300 eggs per year, so we need to nip this in the bud. However, we don't want to take a blunderbuss approach to this matter. The concerns of residents and animal activists are equally important, so a balanced approach is needed."

"Can you give us an idea of how much is being spent to reduce the wild chicken population in New Town?"

"I can tell you that the amount is coming out of the

Town Council's annual budget, but this will not affect other municipal projects in New Town." Edward gave himself an internal fist bump for successfully dodging the question. He had once seen Kimberly reduce a newsmaker to tears in a press conference with her sharp questioning. Edward had contemplated sending the individual in question the contact for his media trainer, but decided against it for fear of making him cry again.

The academic was about to point to another raised hand when James interjected. "Kimberly, thank you for the questions. Edward, if you don't mind, I'm going to answer them in Mandarin, and also add a bit more context for the sake of the Chinese papers." Edward had to make a superhuman effort not to roll his eyes as James spent the next three minutes grandstanding for the cameras. To be fair, it was a superb translation of what Edward had said, with a bit of extra context too. *If he does this for every question, I swear to God I'm going to pick up my mic and smash it over his head*, thought Edward, while maintaining what he thought was a neutral expression. His wife would later tell him that the cameras had caught his resting bitch face, which was turned into a gif within hours.

The reporter from the national broadcaster raised her hand. "Prof Low, Karen Teo from Channel News. Can you tell us what is considered a manageable number for the wild chicken population? Is there a danger that the CTF's measures might drive the wild chickens in New Town into extinction?"

Dear God, the animal activists would never let me off, thought Edward. "Well Karen, I can tell you that we are taking a gradual, step-by-step approach here. The amount of Ovistop used is very carefully measured out and monitored each day. If you think of it as a bicycle going downhill, we can always tap the brakes on this. And to answer your other question, between 75 and 100 chickens would be a good number for New Town. This will have to be regularly monitored, of course, to ensure that the wild chicken population remains in check."

What came next was so unexpected that Edward could not restrain his open-mouthed expression of equal parts amazement and annoyance. "It will remain the Agency's job to maintain the wild chicken population at an acceptable level," said Pat. "I have every confidence that Prof Low will make the right decisions on this." The old-timer folded his arms and leaned back in his chair. Before the rooster crows thrice, thought Edward.

The veteran newspaper reporter raised his hand again. He had been doing so since the start of the presser, and Edward had studiously ignored him. But he was now flapping his arm back and forth like a chicken in attempted flight, which made it difficult to keep up the pretence. Bracing himself, Edward called on the journalist.

"Charles Tong, *National Times*," he announced. He was dressed in his usual sober white long-sleeved shirt – sleeves rolled up to the elbows, of course – with work pass hanging off the end of a lanyard around his neck, neatly tucked into his breast pocket. His pants were dark-coloured and so were the frames of his spectacles. After decades on the job, Charles Tong had had more than one run-in with Edward and other government officials.

"Prof Low, has the task force considered culling the chickens?" There it was, the elephant in the room.

"Well, as I said at the start, we want to resolve this issue in a consultative and humane fashion."

"So is the CTF ruling out culling?"

"Culling will only ever be a last resort when it comes to managing wildlife populations."

"Is there any benchmark that needs to be reached before the CTF will consider culling? For example, if the chicken population hits 500?"

"We have no specific benchmarks, Charles. At this moment, we are confident that our measures will work, and the chicken population will soon be on a downward trend. As I have already said, culling is only a last resort."

"But if there are no benchmarks, then how will the CTF know when to start culling?"

He was being led down a cul-de-sac, like a chicken following a trail of feed into a trap, but Edward refused to take the bait. "We have had extensive discussions with our partners on this and will continue to do so. If there is a need to cull the chickens, we will only do so after the proper consultations, and with the greatest of reluctance."

The queries kept coming. "Prof Low, you have given us details of the measures the CTF has taken to reduce the chicken population. There is clearly a plan and a defined target. Since you have said culling is a last resort, surely there are set criteria that will trigger this?"

The words came out of Edward's mouth before he had a chance to stop himself. "As I have already said, Charles, culling is a last resort that will only be applied after discussions with the relevant stakeholders. I don't know how many times you want me to repeat the same answer."

"Sorry Prof Low, I didn't mean to ruffle any feathers. So does this mean the task force doesn't want to reveal the benchmarks that will trigger culling?"

"Very funny. I am not sure how you managed to draw that conclusion, but you are greatly mistaken." Before Charles could get in another query, Edward added, "Sorry ah, I need to answer questions from other reporters." He called on the youngish-looking reporter to his right, whose question made him feel like screaming. "Uh, Prof Low, can you answer his question?"

Edward clasped his hands tightly together. His face remained impressively deadpan. On the inside, he felt like a drowning man gasping for air. Ignoring the buzzing phone in his trouser pocket, he turned to Charles Tong again and enunciated his words as deliberately and calmly as he could manage. "Thank you for the question, Charles. The CTF meets on a weekly basis and will continue to evaluate the best and most appropriate measures for controlling the wild chicken population in New Town. We have not set any benchmarks or milestones for culling. All options remain on the table."

What, no Chinese translation, James? thought Edward. He knew that the aspiring PS would steer clear of anything controversial. It was a mistake to show his annoyance, but Edward felt he had done a decent enough repair job. In fact, he was almost cock-a-hoop. Despite the stumble, Edward had stuck to his talking points and given little away. He felt good about things. Glancing at his watch, he realised that half an hour had already elapsed. With luck, they could wrap this all up in the next 15 mins.

Kimberly had her hand raised again. Against his better judgement, Edward called on her once more.

Reading off her smartphone, the reporter sent a jolt into the conference room. "Prof Low, I'm being told that there was a mix-up in the drugs. The chickens were administered lycopene, not Ovistop."

Edward's alarm was only exceeded by his confusion. Pat and James seemed equally mystified. He was certain that he had come across lycopene before, but the specifics of the drug and the implications of its usage were trapped in the back of his mind. Edward was not about to ask a reporter for a lesson in lycopene, certainly not when he was surrounded by banks of cameras.

He tried to stall for time. "Would you mind repeating the question, Kimberly?"

"Of course, Prof Low. Can you confirm that the wild chickens in New Town were mistakenly administered lycopene, not Ovistop?"

The academic proceeded as cautiously as if he were crossing a minefield. "Not that we would ask you to reveal your source, but where are you getting this information, Kimberly?"

"I can tell you that it's a reliable source with the relevant knowledge." So it was someone in the Ministry, perhaps even the CTF. But Edward still needed to know what lycopene was for before he could answer the question. His phone going off again, Edward turned to his left but James was studiously refusing to make eye contact. There was little point in asking Pat for help too.

There was a tap on his shoulder. A grim-faced Pat had placed his phone on the table and was pushing it towards him. Shifting his eyes downwards, he saw that there was a text from the PS. Edward stifled a gasp as he took in what it said. "Tell Edward Kimberly is right, chickens were given water with lycopene. It enhances the fertility of roosters. Fed to them two weeks ago." Alongside his mounting horror, Edward remembered that, like him, the PS had studied biology at university.

Edward did not have to take out his phone to realise who had been calling and texting, and he knew that no one could have missed the little exchange between him and Pat. The cameras were going off again. It takes 21 days for an egg to hatch, recalled Edward, his clenched fist gradually tightening as he realised that New Town might be looking at a bumper crop of chicks in another week. A simple search on a smartphone about the properties of lycopene would take a reporter considerably less time.

Edward shuffled his notes, inhaling and exhaling slowly, fighting back a rising tide of nausea. He could feel the curious stares of everyone in the room burning into him. His pulse was accelerating faster than a wild chicken running around New Town. Everyone was waiting for him. But he didn't know what to do.

After an interminable pause, Edward chose his next words carefully. "I'm very sorry Kimberly, but I don't have enough information to answer your questions right now. Please be assured that you will have an answer, and that my staff will be in touch with you on this." He turned to Bambi and caught her eye. Carefully and deliberately, he adjusted his spectacles.

The young woman strode to the space between the panel and the journalists and cleared her throat. "Ladies and gentlemen of the media, we have now come to the end of the press conference. Thank you very much for attending today's briefing. The panel will now take their leave."

Edward got up and walked out of the room as quickly as he could, pausing for the briefest of moments to nod gratefully at Bambi. His fellow panellists hurried after him, barely giving the assembled journalists time to react. Edward knew that the journalists and social media would have a field day with this. But it was the easiest response in the face of difficult questions: walk away and don't say a word.

The CTF panellists did not speak again until they were safely ensconced in a room. Edward shut the door behind him and sank into a nearby chair, finally able to breathe again.

"What happened back there?" asked James. "Why did you end the presser?"

Pat took out his phone and showed it to James. As the light of realisation dawned in James's eyes, the look of sympathy he gave Edward felt genuine for once. "Why didn't we know this," asked Edward plaintively. "How could this happen?" Neither of his fellow task force members had an answer.

"PS wants to see us," said Pat. "He's coming here right now."

"Good loh," said Edward gloomily, staring at the floor. "He can appoint a new chair."

"It will be fine lah," declared Pat, to the utter surprise of his colleagues. There were only MSM outlets there, so we can easily control the narrative. I will ask the comms people to reach out to the editors and get them to hold their stories for now, while we come up with a statement."

"And if they don't?" asked Edward.

"Of course they will," said Pat. "And once I find out who's responsible for this fuck up, and who leaked this to the media, I will hang the both of them." He was already tapping instructions into his phone, sending out WhatsApp messages and emails at a dizzying rate.

Edward and James stared at their colleague. There was life in the old bird yet.

There was a knock at the door. The permanent secretary, a man at least five years younger than Edward, swept into the room with a flourish. He had an air of self-control that Edward had only seen in certain civil servants, mainly the ones at the top of the pecking order. He pulled up a chair and took a seat in front of Edward. "How are you, Ed."

Edward wasn't expecting that to be his first question. "I'm okay. Sorry, PS. I didn't know what else to do," he said weakly.

"You did the right thing."

"I did?"

"Of course you did. If they have no answers, they have no story."

"But what about the footage of us walking out of the room?" Edward could already imagine the gifs of him sitting speechless before the media, playing on repeat and forwarded from one WhatsApp group to the next.

"It will play for a while, but we just need to lay low for now. We can fix this." He turned to Pat. "Pat, can I count on you to find out what went wrong with the Ovistop?"

"Leave it to me, PS."

The permanent secretary's next words startled and delighted Edward in equal measure. "I see you didn't have much to say in the presser, James. You need to do better." Edward only wished he could right click and save the expression of utter consternation on James' face that followed.

The senior civil servant turned his gaze back to Edward. "Focus on getting results. No one can argue with that." His next words made Edward's heart swell. "Always remember who you are ultimately accountable to: the residents of New Town."

"Fuck the media lah," exclaimed Pat with a heartiness that made Edward laugh.

There was just the barest trace of a grin on the permanent secretary's face. "Are you with me, Ed?"

Edward pondered for a moment before he answered. "Yes, PS," he said with a wry smile. "I won't chicken out."

Water Body

The coffin came floating lazily down the Singapore River on a steamy, cloudless Friday afternoon. It meandered past the startled tourists sitting on the old stone steps at the banks and the bemused office workers strolling by.

At first glance, one might have thought it was a long wooden crate, or perhaps some trick of the harsh sunlight that beat down on the glistening waters. But it was exactly what it was: a sarcophagus sailing past the restaurants and bars and pubs that sat above it at Boat Quay. The tide was high, but the current that carried it along was not especially strong. It drifted along the curve of the river, the waves lightly lapping against it.

Out came the smartphones, the onlookers tracking the dark brown wooden box with one hand and wiping the sweat from their brows with the other. It took only minutes before the images and videos they posted went viral. For it was a curious sight indeed in the business district with the shiny, high-rise buildings and burnished monuments all around. The operators of the bumboats that plied their trade up and down the river were on their break, which left the coffin bobbing along by itself.

If the gawking onlookers knew the history of the river, they might have known that, once upon a time, the coffin would not have been so out of place there. Decades ago, it was so polluted with detritus – it was not unusual to see night soil, or even unclaimed bodies, dumped into it – that one could smell the stench from far away. The cleanup began in 1977, and a decade later, the waters were finally pristine. But surely no one thought that they would see a funerary box floating in it one day in the 2020s.

On and on it went, delicately tracing a path in the dark green waters. Where had the coffin come from? Who had dumped it in the river?

There was the other question too: was there really a body in it?

As if on command, it came to a halt at the north bank of Boat Quay, lightly bumping against the stone embankment, just a few metres from the white polymarble statue of the imperious man who stood with his arms folded on a high pedestal, his cool, haughty visage directed towards shore. The more superstitious of the spectators immediately took note of the timing, so that they could buy a 4D ticket later. They also hung around to see if there really was a corpse, for that timing might turn out to be auspicious too. It would not have been a very lucky thing for the unfortunate soul that might be within, but that was no reason they should not strike it rich.

It was a different story for the cleaners and the civil servants summoned by the authorities, who clenched their jaws and said silent prayers to the respective deities they worshipped that the box was empty. Someone had to fish the coffin out of the water, and it certainly wasn't going to be the well-heeled tourists around them.

The morning that followed the extraordinary discovery was as unremarkable as any other. The waters ebbed and flowed with the tide in and out of Boat Quay, while most of the establishments around it were shuttered until their usual opening hours in the evening. Reports about the incident in the less savoury websites tried to outdo each other with their headlines, from "It's alive! Coffin spotted in Singapore River" to "What's in the box? Tourists shocked by floating coffin". Predictably, all the authorities had to say was that the coffin had been "immediately" retrieved from the river and that "investigations are ongoing".

This was the task that had fallen to the three men standing around the coffin, now laid on trestles, in an air-conditioned room in a nondescript government building. One was from the utilities board that oversaw all water resources in the country, another from the police, and the third from the environment agency. They had gathered to determine which ministry had jurisdiction over the box and its contents. Each man fervently hoped it would not be his.

"Why didn't they open it on the spot?" asked Civil Servant Number One. The senior of the bunch, the deputy secretary was a singularly severe man who had spent his entire career in the civil service after winning an overseas scholarship straight out of junior college. The joke among his subordinates was that whenever his children did well in school, they received a terse congratulatory email from him. Handshakes were only for special occasions.

"They didn't have the right tools, DS," replied Civil Servant Number Two, a police superintendent smartly turned out in his dark blue uniform. "They could have cut the coffin open, but they didn't want to take the risk, in case there was really a body inside. And ..."

"And?" asked Number One.

"They were too scared to do it."

"Even our policemen?" said Number One with more than a faint note of disgust in his voice.

"Yes." Number Two had seen his fair share of murders and violent crimes, as well as downright bizarre cases, over the years. The way he saw it, it would not have been all that much of a surprise if a jiangshi were to hop out of the box. But he had seen enough Hong Kong movies to know that even vampires could be killed. His hand instinctively went to the Taoist talisman, specially blessed by a priest, that hung on a necklace around his neck.

"Since we didn't know which ministry should take the lead, we decided to move the coffin to a neutral venue until we were sure," said Civil Servant Number Three, a deputy director and the most junior of the lot. All of them were scholars of some sort, but he ranked bottom of the pecking order, since he had not gone to an overseas university. His mind was filled with stories of water ghosts that his grandmother had told him as a child. These were the spirits of people who had drowned and preyed on unwary swimmers. Suppressing a shudder, Number Three pondered if they had really brought a spirit into the premises. In the old days – and even in the present – a medium might have been called in to chant prayers and drive away the bad spirits.

"Casket."

"Sorry?" said Number Three.

"The correct term is casket," said Number One. "A coffin is tapered at the head and rounded at the shoulders. A casket is rectangular and made of better quality timber. The terms are often used interchangeably, but what we have here is clearly a casket."

"I stand corrected, DS," said Number Three. It was a beautifully constructed casket, carved from mahogany and adorned with decorative corners and brass swing handles. Despite its time in the water, the high gloss finish of its lacquer coat gleamed in the fluorescent light. If there truly was a cadaver in the box, he or she could not have been impoverished in life.

Number One pursed his lips as he thought out loud. "I can't smell anything. That means there's no body, right?"

"Not necessarily," said Number Three. "Most coffins – sorry, caskets – have a rubber gasket. It creates an airtight seal between the lid and the body of the casket, so the smell of the decomposition won't get out."

"I see. Any idea who put it in the water?"

"My officers are combing through the CCTV footages, DS," said Number Two, with the classic civil service penchant for confusing the plural form of certain words. "We canvassed the surrounding areas of the river and the nearby neighbourhoods. Our working theory is that it came down from Alexandra Canal, which feeds the Singapore River. We are also interviewing a person of interest today."

The eyes of the senior man flitted from Number Two to Number Three and back again. It should not have been a terribly difficult matter to handle. After all, drownings in the Singapore River took place on a semi-regular basis, usually because some drunken fool had fallen into it in the dead of night. The bodies were retrieved with a minimum of fuss and routine investigations. But this case had been complicated by the press coverage and the mocking social media posts, which never failed to make the government nervous.

If there was one thing Number One had learned in his long career, it was that the powers that be never liked surprises. They were especially not fond of anything that, in their paranoia, might tarnish their image and, by their reasoning, the image of the country. The permanent secretary of his ministry had now taken a personal interest in the matter, likely on the instructions of the minister. Number One had strict instructions to call the PS once the contents of the casket had been ascertained.

"So," said Number One wryly. "Time to open Pandora's box."

Right on cue, there was a rapping at the door, which made the three men jump involuntarily.

"Come in," said Number One, quickly regaining his composure. A man in his 50s entered the room. He brought with him an air of serenity, as if he dealt with such matters on a daily basis.

"DS, this is Mr Tay. He's the funeral director I told you about," said Number Three. Mr Tay bowed slightly as he shook hands with Number One.

"Mr Tay, will you please open the casket?" said Number Three. From his pocket, the funeral director produced an Allen key. Stepping forward to the base of the casket, he carefully removed the screw there and inserted the key in its place, turning it counterclockwise. The trio of civil servants watched his every move.

Several minutes later, the funeral director was still bent over and fumbling with the key.

"What's wrong?" asked Number One brusquely.

Mr Tay cleared his throat before responding. "Spoil."

"What?"

"Cannot open," he said with a faintly embarrassed air as he straightened up awkwardly.

Number Three cleared his throat. "Maybe Mr Tay just needs the right key?"

"This is the right key," said Mr Tay. "But not working."

"And why not?" asked Number One.

"The coffin in the river very long. Now the lock spoil."

Number One was rapidly running out of patience. "Can you open it or not, Mr Tay?"

It was then that they heard the knock.

Four pairs of eyes turned simultaneously to the wooden box before turning to each other. Seconds later, another knock followed. Then another.

It was unmistakable: the knocks were coming from within the coffin.

No one spoke. None of the quartet dared make eye contact. Their eyes were locked on the wooden box and the secrets that it held. The casket was an unfathomable mystery, and no one dared unearth its secrets.

That afternoon, the investigation officer stopped outside the cramped interview room located in the same government building and scrolled through the notes on his tablet one last time. He was dressed as if he were going to a funeral, with dark tailored pants and black shoes, and a white long-sleeved short rolled up to his elbows. Like an estuary, the task of connecting the various pieces of the puzzle had flowed down to the officer. Or as the cruder of his colleagues might have said, the shit had come to him.

He stepped into the room to be greeted by the sight of a South Asian man in his 20s, seated at a gleaming formica table. His callused hands were clasped before him. He smelled of dried sweat and mud, and the T-shirt and jeans he wore were stained and grimy. He had a gentle way about him.

The officer closed the door and locked it. Once or twice, while he was in the midst of conducting an interview, one of the higher-ups had barged their way in and insisted on observing proceedings. It was a surefire way of frightening the interviewee into either reticence, or a panicked admission to whatever wrongdoing for which they were being investigated. When he spoke to the bosses about it, the specious argument they consistently proffered was that if you had done nothing wrong, you had nothing to fear.

After a decade in the civil service, the officer was a stickler for procedures. But more importantly, he had learned exactly when to stand his ground, and when to plead ignorance in the face of the overbearing. He took a seat across from the man, placing his tablet on the table. He took out his phone and activated the audio recording function.

"Hello."

"Hello, sir," said the man, who could not have been older than 25. The most striking thing about him was his silver irises and sharp, aristocratic features. But his manner was diffident and his smile ever present. He reminded the officer of a model student in school, the kind all the teachers and even fellow students liked. His eyes were remarkable to the officer, who had dealt with hundreds of migrant workers but never seen one with features like his.

"What is your name?"

"Yusuf, sir. Work permit okay, sir. I come Singapore one year. Working construction site lah." He spoke in a low, timorous lilt, and the cadences of his speech sounded remarkably Singaporean. He half expected the young man to break into fluent Singlish. As it was, he had to suppress a grin.

"You don't have to call me sir. My name is Chun Han. We are not here to discuss your work permit."

"Yes, Chun Han, sir. Okay lah."

Chun Han gave up. Employment passes did not even come under his remit, but Chun Han still wielded enormous power over the man across the table. It made him deeply uncomfortable to think about it.

"Where are you from, Yusuf?" It had become a habit of late for Chun Han to ask questions to which he already knew the answers. He was no interrogator, but he found that the process of questioning set the interviewee at ease.

"From Dhaka, sir. 4,320 kilometres."

"You even know the distance," remarked Chun Han. "You've come a long way."

"Tagore say: cannot cross sea by staring at water lah."

"You like poetry?" Chun Han had met enough Bangladeshis to know that even among blue collar workers, there was a strong appreciation for the Bengali language and literature. Many of them often turned out to be university students who had dropped out to find work in Singapore.

"I am poet," said Yusuf with evident pride. "Five newspaper publish me. Singapore, *Banglar Kantha* also publish me," he added, referring to the local Bengali newspaper that catered to the thousands of Bangladeshi workers in the country. His smile had gotten even wider.

"What do you write about?"

"Love. Family. Death." His chin dipped. "Singapore, I work construction."

"I see," said Chun Han. "Yusuf, do you know why you are here?"

"Don't know, sir. Boss tell me come, I come." He continued beaming at Chun Han.

Chun Han picked up his tablet and scrolled to a news report about the casket, which included a large photo of several men hoisting it out of the river. "Have you seen this?"

Yusuf glanced over at the tablet. "Yes, my friends tell me."

"What did you think of it?"

Yusuf pondered the question. "Strange, sir."

"Strange, indeed," said Chun Han, who tapped his tablet

several more times. Turning the screen towards Yusuf, he scrolled through several grainy CCTV images. They showed two men carrying what appeared to be a large wooden crate out of a void deck. "Is that you?"

The Bangladeshi studied the photos carefully. "Yes, sir."

"Who is that man with you?"

"Mr Tang, sir. Very nice man."

Chun Han noted the time stamp on the photos again. The two men had been captured in the early hours of Friday morning. "How do you know Mr Tang?"

"I meet him at canal. Alexandra Canal. I finish work, walk there every day."

"You finished work in the morning?"

"Overnight shift, sir."

"Is he your friend?"

"I meet him at canal," repeated Yusuf.

"What was he doing there?"

"He sit there, he crying. Very sad. I ask him, okay?"

"And what did he say?"

"He say, father die. Funeral start, going to cremate. Very sad, sir. I sit with him, make sure he okay."

"I see," said Chun Han. He was watching Yusuf's reactions carefully. He could not sense anything deceitful about him. But that did not mean he had nothing to hide.

"So sad, sir." The way Yusuf spoke, unhurried and languorous, reminded Chun Han of sitting at the beach on a sunny day. Or taking a long ride down the river. Either way, Chun Han sat back and let him set the pace. There was no need to rush him.

"Yes, that is sad."

"I think of father, more sadder."

"Do you mean your own father?"

"Yes, sir."

"Is he back home in Dhaka?"

"I come Singapore, he die," said Yusuf, his head down.

"I'm very sorry to hear that, Yusuf."

"Cancer. Mother say, don't come back. She say, work hard, money for family. Brother, sister, all need me."

"Are you the eldest?"

"Yes. Number one, brother, sister. Sister seventeen."

"Were you close to your father?"

Yusuf took a long pause before responding. "Yes."

"My condolences, Yusuf."

"I am university student."

"I'm sorry?"

"I am university student," repeated Yusuf. "In Dhaka. Literature department. Professor say I am top student." He added wistfully, "But mother say, come Singapore work. Make money for family."

Chun Han could hear raised voices beyond the door. He ignored them and pressed on. "What else did Mr Tang say?"

"He say, he have beautiful coffin. $10,000. Family tell him, don't buy. But he buy. He say, I have money, no father. I want father, no money." Blinking as if in slow motion, Yusuf shifted his gaze towards Chun Han. "He say, help me."

Chun Han picked up his tablet. He scrolled to the last of the CCTV images, which showed the two men lifting up the crate and pushing it into a canal. "Is this what Mr Tang asked you to do?"

"Yes, sir."

"Why?"

"Father like sea. Father like boat. He say last time young, father take him sailing. Go Pulau Ubin, Malaysia. Very fun." Chun Han waited as Yusuf gathered his thoughts. "He say, give father last journey. For ritual."

"Last journey?"

"Sailing journey."

"So he asked you to help him throw a coffin in the canal?" asked Chun Han in disbelief. From outside the room came the chatter again, as if a quarrel was taking place. It was a constant problem in an old building where the walls were thin and even whispered conversations might be overheard. Chun Han was tempted to stick his head out the door and tell whoever it was to keep it down. But he didn't. Instead, he continued listening to Yusuf. The end of the journey was nigh.

"I no understand, sir," said Yusuf. "I say, go sea, throw father ashes. But Mr Tang, he crying crying crying. He say, family no help. I think he …" he faltered, pointing to his temple.

"Crazy?"

"Yes. Crazy. But so sad. So I help."

"Where did you carry it from?"

"Mr Tang take me to void deck. Nearby."

"What happened after you went there?"

"Priest come."

"Priest?"

"Yes."

"Say prayer. Put yellow paper, flowers. Pour blood."

"Pour blood?"

"Yes. Mr Tang cut hand. Open coffin, pour blood. Priest pray. He say, so father don't wake up."

"Wake up?"

Yusuf gazed at Chun Han. He wasn't smiling anymore. "Wake up. Come home."

"So the two of you threw the coffin in the canal?"

"Yes, sir."

Chun Han was perplexed. He had attended many funerals and seen plenty of elaborate rituals, be they Buddhist, Taoist, Hindu or Christian. But he had never heard of anyone cutting themselves in order to drip blood on a corpse, or putting a coffin in the river. There were plenty of sea burials, but those only involved scattering ashes. He suspected that the "priest" was no ordained clergy, but some sort of quack purporting to offer services in the occult.

The voices outside the room were getting louder, and closer too. Was someone having a birthday celebration, or some farewell party for a departing colleague? Chun Han didn't care either way, for he was focused on closing the case. There was something about Yusuf's affable ways that made Chun Han want to put his arm around him and tell him that everything would be all right. But he knew that was not strictly true. Did the young worker even know that what he had done was illegal? Everything hinged on the answer to his next question.

"What was in the coffin?"

"Very beautiful. Shiny. Nice to touch."

"Yusuf, please look at me." The Bangladeshi turned his face upwards. "What was in the coffin?"

Yusuf did not break eye contact as he responded. "Mr Tang father."

"You saw a body in it?"

"Yes. Mr Tang father."

Chu Han pondered this. "How did his father die?"

"Mr Tang say father attack. Bite."

"I'm sorry? His father attacked him?"

"No. Something attack father."

"Something attacked him?"

"Mr Tang say …" Yusuf searched for the word. "Jiangshi."

"Mr Tang's father was bitten by a jiangshi?"

"Yes, sir."

Chun Han's mind was reverberating with words like "paranoid schizophrenia" and "hallucinations". No one in their right mind would believe their parents had been murdered by vampires, much less think a coffin could be thrown into a canal without anyone noticing. A more logical explanation was that the so-called Mr Tang was making it all up. He had killed his own father and sought to prey on the gullibility of a kind-hearted soul. For all he knew, the body might not even be that of his father.

He knew that the police had been searching the area near Alexandra Canal but had yet to locate him. He made a mental note to get in touch with his blue-uniformed counterpart and update her on what he had been told. The suspect could well be violent and dangerous. "Did you believe him?"

"Don't know, sir. Don't know jiangshi."

"Were you scared when he told you this?"

"Yes, sir."

Chun Han forged ahead. They were almost at the end game, but he needed to know the truth. "How did the body look?"

"Sorry, sir?"

"The body. Did it have any injuries?"

Yusuf pointed to the side of his neck. "Here. Got hole. Small hole."

"I see." Chun Han pondered for a bit. "Did Mr Tang pay you to help him?"

"He want to pay. $200. I don't take."

"Why not?"

"Don't want."

"Why not?" repeated Chun Han.

Yusuf's beautiful eyes welled up. "I think of father."

A piercing scream came from outside the door, followed by a loud thump. The two men froze. There were ripping, tearing noises emanating from the exterior, as if someone was tearing up cardboard.

Chun Han got up and was about to move to the door when Yusuf grabbed his arm, startling him.

"Don't," said the young worker hoarsely, furiously shaking his head.

The noises came to a halt. Neither Chun Han nor Yusuf dared move a muscle. Their eyes were fixed on the door. A thin puddle of blood, dark and shimmery, gradually flowed into the room beneath it.

"I think," said Yusuf faintly. "Mr Tang father come back."

It started with a faint scratching at the door that was only just audible at first. The doorknob rattled. Light, almost casually, before it got progressively louder. Soon, there was a furious banging at the door.

The faithful civil servant and the frightened migrant worker sat there, paralysed by a fear that reached deep into their bones. For it was only a matter of time before the door opened and the late Mr Tang found his way in, and they would both discover their fate.

The Runner

"Are you listening to me, Shaun?"

The runner's surroundings came back into focus once more, and he could feel the weight of the cold steel around his wrists. Around him in the dock sat several of his fellow accused, dressed in purple jumpsuits or, like him, red polo tees and dark blue bermudas. The former were already serving their sentences, while the latter were being remanded as they awaited the outcomes of their respective cases. Between their snores and disinterested expressions, Shaun couldn't tell the difference between the two classes of prisoners. It was his first time in court. The judge, like most of her peers, was already fashionably late.

Shaun caught his lawyer's stern gaze and sat up straight. "Yes, Ms Rajah," he replied dutifully, rubbing his hands together. With the air conditioning on full blast, it felt like sitting in a freezer.

Even at the best of times, Court 26 at the Subordinate Courts often resembled a wet market on a Sunday morning. Through the glass partitions that separated legal proceedings from everyone else, Shaun could see frazzled mothers with toddlers in tow in the public gallery. They were seated alongside elderly men and women who had shuffled to their seats, often while holding onto a cane, and were dozing off from the strain of getting there. Tattooed teenagers swiped through TikTok on their phones, sometimes taking selfies despite the prominent NO PHOTOS sign at the entrance. The bailiffs had long ceased to enforce the rule, unless a judge caught them in the act and ordered them to stop.

There couldn't have been more than a few dozen people in attendance, but the poor acoustics of the courtroom bounced the sound everywhere. Once the hearings started, it was practically impossible to hear what the judge and the lawyers were saying. The chaos of the courtroom startled Shaun, who had only ever seen such places in movies. It reminded him of the one time he attended an S-League match, where there were less than a hundred people present. He half-expected vendors hawking nasi lemak and soft drinks to appear.

Directly ahead of Shaun sat the interpreters with their laptops and desktops and digital dictionaries, chatting with one another as they waited for something to do. A few metres off to his right, the prosecutors busied themselves over their laptops, occasionally referring to thick files piled beside them. The reporters in the media section on the other side of the courtroom flipped through stacks of charge sheets, looking for interesting cases they could write about. They reminded him of students going through their lecture notes. Their numbers had been growing over the past hour, each new journalist entering the courtroom through a side door with a booming creak worthy of a horror movie. Shaun wondered which reporter would write a story about him. He suspected it was all of them.

"Please repeat what I told you." The lawyer from the pro bono Criminal Legal Aid Scheme reminded him of a schoolteacher, with her horn-rimmed glasses and severe black-and-white outfits. The surgical mask she wore, a requirement even in the waning days of the pandemic, didn't help. Since the judge hadn't arrived, she was free to approach the dock and confer with her client. Not everyone around Shaun had the luxury of a lawyer. Some foolishly chose to represent themselves. Others did not contest their charges, resigning themselves to a jail term handed down by a judge who knew little about them beyond a charge sheet and a statement of facts.

Shaun had to resist the urge to raise his hand before speaking to the lawyer, even though she wasn't all that much older than him. Ms Rajah spoke in somewhat condescending tones and had a tendency to nag. But the lawyer had a kindly air about her, and he knew that she had a genuine desire to help. Annoying as it was, Shaun couldn't fault her for continually asking him to repeat what she had said, since even he had to admit that he had trouble absorbing instructions. He noted too the way that she had spoken to his elderly mother at length about his case, patiently explaining the procedures that they would have to follow. So he beat down his more rebellious instincts and told himself to treat her with the same respect that she gave his mother.

"When my case number comes up, the clerk will call out my name. I stand up, and the judge will ask me how I intend to plead. I will answer her and she will set a date for the next hearing. After that, they will take me back to remand."

"How do you address the judge?"

"Your Honour."

"Should you say anything to defend yourself when it's your turn?"

"No, I should save it for my trial. You have already prepared the …" He struggled to recall the term she had used.

"Mitigation plea."

"Yes, you will take care of that."

"And what do you do if you have to wait a long time?"

"Don't fall asleep. If the judge sees me like that, it might affect my case."

"Very good. Remember ah, all this is just administrative. Hopefully, we will get an early hearing date for you." Her features softened. "I spoke to your mother just now. She's very worried about you."

Shaun clenched his jaw. He had asked his mother not to come to court, on account of her bad knee. But the truth was that he had already broken her heart the instant she saw him in the detention centre. There was no need to stomp on the pieces.

"What did you tell her?"

"I said I will take care of your case, and everything will be okay."

Shaun didn't want to ask the question, but he had to know. "Did my father call?" The lawyer shook her head and Shaun did his best not to react. He had been expecting it, but it was still difficult to hide his disappointment.

"You see the journalists over there?" She inclined her head ever so slightly to the right. Shaun had already seen a few of them pointing at him and whispering to each other.

"Yes."

"By the end of the day, there will probably be a few stories about you circulating on social media, because your case is so," she said, grasping for the appropriate word, "unusual. Don't pay any attention to them. Just remember that what goes viral today will be forgotten tomorrow."

"Yes, Ms Rajah. Thank you for helping me."

"You are very welcome, Shaun. We will get through this, okay?"

"Bangun, all rise." The court – or about half of it, at any rate – rose to their feet at the bailiff's command. Ms Rajah scurried back to the defence lawyers' table near the reporters, while the judge made her way to her place, elevated above everyone else. She paused briefly as the court bowed, and the magistrate took her seat.

"Hello? Can you all hear me? Raise your hand or say something if you can."

Twelve months before his debut court appearance, Shaun sat at the grimy staircase of a HDB block and stared at his phone, straining to hear the Zoom call through his secondhand earphones. There was a stench of urine in the air. Obscene graffiti was scrawled on the walls, while cockroaches scuttled across the ground. It had taken forever to find an unsecured Wi-Fi network that he could tap into, and this was the spot where the signal was strongest. It was also a place where the red-shirted social distancing ambassadors would never come.

There was no router in the miniscule one-room rental flat that he shared with his mother, and he didn't want her to overhear what was being said. But in any case, he needed to get out and about. Being forced to stay home during the lockdown was driving him mad, along with his mother's constant nagging to get a job. His father had long left the family, taking Shaun's older sister with him. He could still remember the old man's words as he stalked off. "Don't call me Daddy. You're the greatest disappointment of my life."

In the years since, he had often thought about what exactly a six-year-old could have done to disappoint an adult so. The only conclusion Shaun could come to was that his father hated him the moment he emerged from his mother's womb and took his first breath.

With his mother in ill health, Shaun had little choice but to be the breadwinner. But there were slim pickings for poly dropouts, and the pandemic made everything worse. Normal life had come to a halt, but the bills didn't. He was reduced to doing odd jobs like assisting at hawker stalls or taking food and drink orders in a kopitiam, but even those were out now, given the number of complaints by irate customers annoyed by his inability to remember their orders. Like everyone else, Shaun had also tried his hand at being a delivery rider, but he was let go within a week as he couldn't make his deliveries on time. He was perpetually guilty of those magic words: having an attitude. It was a phrase whose meaning he was still unable to divine.

Shaun could see that there were 15 people on the call, but almost all of them had switched off their cameras at Larry's insistence. "I don't want to see your face and you don't want to see mine," he had said as they logged in. This did not stop one or two from using avatars like cats and rabbits, a dead giveaway for their demographic. Shaun had been referred to Larry by a former classmate who sent him the Zoom link. All he had said was that it was an easy way to make money on one's own time.

A chorus of raised hands lit up the screen. "Okay, let's start," said Larry. He spoke in oddly soothing tones, like a deejay, or a sleep app. "Let me make it very simple for everyone. I lend people money. Sometimes, they don't pay up. That's why I need all of you to help me give them some encouragement."

Shaun laughed out loud at "encouragement", as if they were applying to be preschool teachers.

"Each time you encourage someone to pay me back, I will pay you. You also get a bonus if they pay up quickly. Any questions?"

No one said a word, whether out loud or in the chat. It didn't surprise Shaun in the slightest that he was being recruited to an illegal enterprise. He knew friends who had been loan shark runners, and they all told him that it was good money. Like food delivery and transport gig workers, runners worked on a commission basis. But unlike Grab or Deliveroo, you didn't have to give your paymasters a cut for each job you did.

"Doesn't anyone want to know what this involves?" asked Larry with a chuckle. Some had already given their answer by dropping off the call, until there were only seven of them left. Anyone capable of doing a Google search would know what loan shark runners did. But that was not the most important question.

The cat avatar, standing against a backdrop of swaying green fields, was moving its mouth but nothing could be heard. "You're on mute," said Larry.

"How much?" said the feline. To Shaun's surprise, it was a girl's voice.

"Depending on the job, $300 to $500 each time. Payment in cash. Every week, I will send out a list of assignments. You pick the ones you want to do. Each job has a deadline. If you don't complete it on time, you won't get the full payment."

"What do we need to do?" asked a disembodied voice from a black square.

"Leave a message."

"What kind of message?"

"If you decide you want to work for me, someone will brief you on what to do. How much you get will depend on the kind of message."

It was the rabbit avatar's turn to speak. "Do we have to," the rabbit's ears flopped here and there as it dithered. "Hurt anyone?"

Larry sniggered. "No lah, this is not that kind of job. You go to their house, you leave the message, you take photos, you leave. That's it."

"Then if police come leh?"

"Then that's your own dai ji loh. But if you do it well, I will give you more. The more jobs you do, the more money I pay you."

The shadows cast by the setting sun were gradually lengthening on the staircase where Shaun sat. Despite the virtual setting, you could practically hear the gears turning in everyone's heads as they did their mental sums.

"So how? Want not?" asked Larry genially.

It was well past midnight when Shaun found himself at another staircase, this time at an estate far from home, one that was considerably more upmarket than his own. It had taken almost an hour to get there, with a train and change of two buses. He had taken off his mask and fastened it on his right bicep, so he could breathe easier. His ragged backpack on his shoulders, Shaun glanced at the small, blue pail beside him. It had taken a long time, and considerable effort, to fill it. He had sealed it as best as he could with tin foil and plastic and buried it in his backpack under some rags, to keep the smell at bay.

The list of jobs Larry sent out in the Telegram group, comprising the seven who had stayed on the Zoom call, were quickly snapped up. They could choose their assignments – fastest fingers first – but only up to a point: Larry insisted on giving them jobs far from where they lived, in order to avoid detection. Shaun quickly learned that the level of harassment each home was subjected to was based on how much they owed Larry, who only ever sent messages that self-destructed within a day and insisted that they do the same. He also found out that some of his new colleagues were themselves in debt to Larry, and this was a means of paying it off, bit by bit.

There were three categories of jobs – A, B and C – with increasing levels of pay based on the difficulty of the assignment. Scrawling messages on the external walls of homes and fastening their grille gates with bicycle locks belonged to Category A and got you $300. Category B comprised the time-honoured practice of hanging a pig's head – preferably a rotting one – accompanied by liberal splashing of paint or kerosene on a residential door. Sometimes, it also involved scrawling messages at the lift lobby, so that more neighbours knew about their debt, and the humiliation was doubled. For this, Larry paid $400. Each runner would do the deed, then take photos of the aftermath and send them to Larry over Telegram.

They were each given a budget to buy the necessary materials. Receipts had to be kept – reimbursement for what they had spent would only be given once the job was done. They were told time and again to only carry out their assignments at night and to wear a mask, which was not an issue in pandemic times. They were also to leave the scene immediately once they were done. Above all, they were to keep their mouths shut about Larry if they were caught. "If you say too much, maybe I will also have to send you some encouragement," he said with a chuckle.

Then there was Category C. Larry had explained the first two categories over Telegram, but would only talk about the third over individual phone calls to those who picked them. As was his wont, he got straight to the point over the line with Shaun. "You have to put shit on the door."

"What?"

"I need you to go and get some shit, and smear it on the door," said Larry. "The more shit, the better."

Shaun was reeling. "What … what kind of shit?"

"Any kind will do. You want to make it yourself, also can. Just make sure you take photos," said Larry.

"That's fucking gross lah," exclaimed Shaun.

"Yes. That's why I'm paying you $500."

"Can I use piss?"

"Cannot. Not for this job."

"Why not?"

"This one owes me a lot of money. Need to teach him a lesson. But if you want, you can also pee on his door."

Shaun went quiet.

"Still want to do it not?" asked Larry. His mild tone never wavered. Listening to his voice, you would never have imagined him capable of dispatching runners to harass debtors. Shaun pictured him as a mild-mannered uncle, patiently giving clear instructions to his charges and guiding them along. In another life, Larry might have made a good teacher. Or maybe he was just a sociopath.

Shaun thought of his mother and the unpaid bills that were stacking up by the day. He gritted his teeth. "I'll do it."

Crouching at the top of the staircase and peeking round the corner, Shaun looked at the pail beside him again. How long had he been waiting there? He couldn't tell if several minutes or an hour had passed. Shaun took out his phone and checked the screenshot of Larry's message for the address again. It was the unit at the end of the corridor, the one with a crucifix hanging on the door and two tricycles parked outside. It was now or never.

He took out a pair of plastic gloves from his backpack and put them on. Placing his mask back on, Shaun picked up the pail and tore off the foil and plastic. He walked gingerly to the unit, reaching it in a matter of seconds. Carefully placing the pail to one side, he was relieved to see that there were no CCTVs in sight. The crucifix, however, gazed down upon him with an unnerving air. Shaun was not religious, but it still made him uneasy.

"Forgive me, Jesus," he whispered, before reaching into his backpack and pulling out a can of spray paint. Shaking it vigorously, he sprayed the large signs, OP, in bright red characters on the wall beside the door. He put the can down and steadied himself for the real task at hand.

Reaching deep into the pail, Shaun grimaced and grabbed a handful of the brown stuff. The runner proceeded to smear it on the grille gate, making sure to get more of it on the keyhole, as Larry had instructed. He reached into the pail again and grabbed more before reaching between the gaps in the gate and smearing it on the door. It only took a couple of minutes before he ran out of material. Shaun gingerly peeled the gloves off, placing them carefully inside the pail. He took out his phone and snapped a few photos. The deed was done.

The runner stepped back and pondered a moment. Larry's words rang in his head: "Must teach him a lesson."

Shaun unzipped his bermudas and proceeded to urinate all over the threshold of the unfortunate flat. He knew nothing about the residents or their circumstances. But for reasons he couldn't explain, it felt good to piss all over them. Shaun zipped up. Then he picked up his equipment and took off, disappearing into the night.

"Where were you on the 26th of April around midnight?" Sitting in the air-conditioned interview room, Shaun stifled a shiver. He had been in there for more than an hour and a half.

The police had come knocking a month after his first assignment, politely requesting his presence at the station. Before they got to him, he had done more than his fair share of encouragement for Larry, scrawling messages and splashing paint aplenty. Shaun found himself enjoying the work. It was simple, provided you did it swiftly and kept to the instructions. Payment always came quickly too. But despite Larry's offer of more money, he had declined to do any more Category C jobs. Once was more than enough.

"How many times must I tell you?"

"Just one more time, please," said the middle-aged officer across the table from him, an apologetic smile plastered to his face. He had asked the same question three times now. Shaun took an instant dislike to him. He reminded him of his father, with his bushy moustache and short-sleeved shirt. They were supposed to be wearing masks, but this requirement didn't seem to bother the officer.

"Where were you on the 26th of April?" repeated the officer.

"I was at Orchard." Shaun had named the first place that came to mind without thinking about whether it made sense, or how far it was from home.

"What were you doing?"

"Walking around loh."

"At midnight? All the malls are closed."

"I was bored. Nothing to do."

"The lockdown is still on. Why didn't you stay home?"

"Like I said, bored loh."

"Who were you with?"

"No one."

"Where did you go?"

"Wisma. Orchard Central. Everywhere."

"Can you be more specific? You went to Wisma, Orchard Central and?" The officer was laboriously taking notes in longhand, and it was making Shaun restless. He had done that each time he repeated a question to Shaun. He wondered why he couldn't just use a laptop.

"I just walked down from Ion. Can't remember all the places."

"Okay." The scratching of the officer's pen on paper filled the air.

"How long is this going to take? Can I go home now?"

The officer ignored the question. "So if I send my officers to all these places to look at the CCTV footage, they will see you, yeah?" The abrupt nature of the query caught Shaun off guard, but he recovered sufficiently to nod his head vigorously.

"What time did you go to town?"

"About 8pm, I think."

"Can you tell me which shops you went to? So we know where to look."

Shaun had not been to any of the malls he mentioned in ages. "I can't really remember. I have to think about it."

"No problem," said the officer, beaming again. "How did you get home after that?"

"Walk loh. No more trains or buses."

"All the way back to Cantonment?"

"Yeah."

"You must be very fit."

"I do it all the time."

"Nice. Did you go anywhere near Bedok when you went home?"

"Bedok? No lah. So far." Shaun's pulse was speeding up. That was where the vandalised unit was located.

"You sure?"

"Yes, I'm sure."

"Okay." The officer picked up a tablet and propped it up on its stand, turning it towards Shaun. He tapped it a few times and a grainy black and white photograph materialised. It showed a man sitting in the middle of a staircase, a backpack on his shoulders and a small pail beside him. He was staring upwards. Despite the poor lighting, it was recognisably Shaun.

"Is this you?"

He made a show of looking intently at the image. "No, it's not me."

"You sure?"

"It's not me lah," he snapped, before composing himself. "I already told you I didn't go to Bedok."

"Could it be your twin brother? You don't have a twin, do you?"

Shaun couldn't tell if the officer was joking or not. "No, I have a sister."

"I see." The officer inhaled deeply as he put the tablet down. His expression suggested that he was pondering

Shaun's words deeply, as if he had uttered some profound truth. "You know what?"

"What?"

"I never told you that this photo was taken in Bedok."

"What?"

"I never told you that this photo was taken in Bedok," said the officer again.

"I just guessed loh." Shaun was sweating despite the chill. He wanted to go home.

"Lucky guess?"

"Yes! I'm telling the truth!"

"All right, Shaun. I believe you." The perpetual hum of the air-conditioning was like a third person in the room. It was comforting and unnerving all at once. "Do you know a man named Larry?"

"I don't know any Larry." Shaun's heart pounded away in his chest, the accompanying soundtrack to the predicament he found himself in.

The officer picked up the tablet and tapped it again. Screenshots of Larry's conversations with the Telegram group appeared. He scrolled through them at a leisurely pace, as if he were showing off his holiday photos. It was all there: details of the three categories of jobs, payment, instructions and more.

"This is a Telegram group started by Larry. He's a loan shark, and he uses it to assign runners," said the officer. "I can see texts from a Shaun here. Is this you?"

For the first time in his life, Shaun understood what it meant to have his blood turn cold. Someone in the group chat must have talked already.

"Shaun?" The steady persistence of the officer was beginning to grate on him. He was like a dog with the bit between his teeth. At any moment, he would pounce on Shaun and tear him to pieces. "Is this you?"

"No."

"You sure?"

"Yes! How many times you want to ask me?"

"I'm sorry, Shaun. I need to be sure. It's my job," said the officer sheepishly. "So if I ask you to take out your phone and show me your Telegram chats, I won't see the same messages?"

Shaun was in full panic mode now. Most of the messages had self-destructed but he realised that he still had screenshots that he had forgotten to delete. "You have no right to see my phone. I will sue you!"

"I don't need your permission, Shaun. I can take it from you if I think you've committed a crime." There was a much harder edge to the officer's tone now. "I need you to listen to me, Shaun. Can you do that?"

Shaun nodded numbly. He stared at the table, as if the answers were going to magically appear there.

"You don't have any witnesses who can vouch that you were in Orchard last month. I can send my men to go to the places that you mentioned, but there's no need to. I know you didn't go there."

Shaun didn't respond, but the officer went on. "We have CCTV footage of you in Bedok. We have screenshots of the Telegram chat. And I'm very sure if I look at your phone, I will see the same messages."

Shaun knew that the game was up, but he couldn't quite bring himself to acknowledge it. He felt like he was drowning.

"Are you listening to me, Shaun?"
"Yes."
"Are you ready to tell me the truth now?"
Shaun nodded faintly several times.
"Did you go to the Bedok flat last month?"
"Yes."
"What did you do there?"
Shaun exhaled. He was finally finding his voice. "I sprayed OP on the wall."
"What's that?"
"I sprayed OP on the wall," said Shaun again, his voice weak and strained.
"Why did you do that?"
Shaun recalled Larry's threatening words as an afterthought. There seemed little point in hiding anything from the officer now. "Because Larry asked me to. The people there owe him money."
"And what did you get for spraying that on the wall?"
"$500."
"How did Larry communicate with you?"
"Telegram loh. You saw it already."
"Did Larry ask you to do anything else?"
"I put shit on the door."
"What was that like?"
Shaun stared at the officer in disbelief. "It was fucking gross, can."
The officer suppressed a smirk. It was the expression of a man who already knew the answers to all the questions he was asking. "You know ah, Shaun, I don't think I could do what you did."

"No choice. My mother can't work. We need the money. There's no one to help."

"What about your father and sister?"

"I don't know where they are."

"I see." The officer softened his tone. "So where did you get the shit from?"

"It's not shit."

"I'm sorry?"

"It's not shit," he repeated.

"It's not?"

"It's chocolate."

The officer guffawed. "Chocolate?"

"Yes, chocolate. Plus kaya and green tea."

"It's a mixture of chocolate, kaya and green tea?"

"Yes. You can go and test it if you don't believe me."

"So instead of using shit, you made … fake shit?"

"Yes."

"From chocolate, kaya and green tea."

"Yes."

"Larry was okay with this?"

"Larry didn't know."

"Wah."

"It's damn gross lah. I'm not going to put shit on my hands. Not even if you pay me $10,000."

The officer could not contain his laughter now. With considerable effort, he composed himself. "Where did you get the materials from?"

"Around my house. It's all expired. I just used whatever I could find. I mixed it up and I left it overnight, so that it will stink."

"So you made fake shit without telling Larry, and you put it on the door."

"Yes."

"And got $500 for it."

"Yes." There was nothing more to be said. He was at the mercy of the police, and they knew everything now. Shaun realised that the officer was no longer taking notes.

"I need to tell you something, Shaun," said the officer, breaking the stillness.

"What?"

"Fake shit or not, you still committed a crime."

Shaun's head was bowed. "I know."

"You traumatised that family, and we will ask them to press charges. And you're going to go to jail."

The young runner did not have a response for the police officer. He simply sat there, head bowed, contemplating how he had become the greatest disappointment of his father's life.

The Queen of Heaven

It is said that on a certain day of a certain month in certain years, something unusual happens at the Grand Mazu Temple in the West Central District of Tainan, Taiwan.

The Grand Mazu Temple was once the palace of the 17th-century royal, Zhu Shugui. The so-called Prince of Ningjing was the last of the pretenders to the throne of the Southern Ming, and had fled to Taiwan as the Qing dynasty was established. But in 1683, his forces were comprehensively defeated by the Manchus as they annexed Taiwan. Crushed by despair, Zhu is said to have told his five concubines, "Now all is lost, and the day of my death is set."

It was a scene fit for a grand opera. The prince sat upon his throne, dressed in his finest robes and surrounded by the ladies who had devoted their lives to him. There wasn't much time left, for the sounds of galloping hooves and clashing swords were coming ever closer. A faithful manservant, the only one left of the legions who once served Zhu Shugui, proffered a silken cord. With trembling hands, he took it and turned his gaze upwards, mutely imploring Heaven for mercy. But in the next moment, the most senior of the ladies stepped forward. With outstretched hand, she too asked for a cord for herself and her sisters.

And so the prince, along with the five consorts who loved him so, hanged himself from the roof beams in his palace.

Unlike other invaders who might have razed it to the ground, the Manchus spared the palace. In 1684, it was converted into a temple dedicated to the sea goddess Mazu, as the Emperor Kangxi conferred the title of Queen of Heaven upon her. Known by 36 names, Mazu oversees all living beings with the help of her guardian generals, the demons Qianliyan (All-seeing) and Shunfeng'er (All-hearing). While she is the patron of sailors and coastal communities, all may call on her. Many miracles have been attributed to her, from the ending of epidemics to the driving out of demons.

There are other gods honoured in the temple too, such as Yue Lao, the god of marriage and love, who is often depicted as an old man standing beneath the moon. But it is the golden visage of Mazu, resplendent in her royal gown and crown of nine beaded tassels, who reigns supreme as she holds the ceremonial tablet of knowledge before her. Above her hangs an elaborately woven banner with one of her titles: Tian Shang Sheng Mu, the Holy Heavenly Mother.

Today, the temple is a magnificent edifice wedged between old and new buildings, a magnet for tourists and devotees alike. But there is someone else to be found in the house of worship.

She sits in a quiet corner of the temple, dozing the day away. Her hair is white as snow, and her lined countenance is reminiscent of the trails left by vehicles passing through the desert. She seems to have emerged straight from a Chinese period drama. One might think she has been at the temple since the beginning. She does not appear to have a name, for she is known simply as the Storyteller. The perennial refrain from those in the know to all visitors is: "Look for the old woman, and ask her to tell you the tale of Lin and Sister Mei."

The Storyteller charges a hundred Taiwanese dollars, but it is money well spent. For once the note crosses her palms, she is transformed. She springs to life, her posture upright and her voice loud and authoritative. A crowd inevitably forms when she utters the words that have become familiar to regular visitors: "Listen carefully. I shall tell this story only once. For not all are meant to hear it, and even fewer to understand it."

Her introduction is uttered as solemnly as a prayer to Mazu. "It is a story of longing and loss, of forbidden love, and Mazu's grace and mercy, which will redeem us all in Heaven's eyes."

On an evening in the ancient past, a young man named Lin made his way to the Grand Mazu temple. He had come to pay obeisance and to ask Mazu's blessings for a long sea journey he was about to undertake. For Lin was an only child whose parents had recently passed, leaving him nothing but the tiny house they lived in. Despite years of study and an arduous journey to the capital, he had also failed the imperial examination. There was nothing left for him in Tainan, and he sought his fortune in Nanyang, the vast expanse of lands beyond China in the south.

Kneeling before the goddess with his hands clasped before him, Lin looked up and contemplated Mazu's sombre expression, her eyelids drooping ever so slightly. He did not truly know if the power of Mazu was real. But he found going to the temple greatly comforting. The Lady of Luminous Grace reminded him of his own mother, who would sit him in her lap and tell him stories of the great goddess and her wondrous deeds.

Once, Mazu was human, a woman of great virtue named Lin Moniang from the city of Meizhou. His mother would sometimes tease him with the prospect that they might be kinsmen with her.

One day, a Taoist master named Xuantong came to her while she was still a child and gave her a book of magical knowledge. By the time she was 13, she had gained supernatural powers through her mastery of the tome. Some said that she saved her family from a typhoon at the age of 16. Others told the story of how she would stand on the shore, clothed in red, to guide fishing boats home in inclement weather. She died young, her virtue intact, and ascended to heaven as a goddess.

Bless me, Ah Ma, Lin muttered as he genuflected the requisite three times and kowtowed another nine times. Help me to bring my parents honour, that they may be proud of me in the afterlife. Grant me a safe journey and success in my endeavours.

As he raised his head, a floral fragrance filled the air, as if a bouquet of freshly bloomed flowers had been laid before him. The very next thing he saw was a woman kneeling beside him in a glistening blue silk tunic, offering her devotions to the Holy Heavenly Mother.

She was unlike any other woman he had ever seen before. She had almond-shaped eyes that twinkled, as if she held a secret that no one else knew. Her skin was as fair as the moonlight, her full lips a shade of bright crimson. And when he saw her smile, replete with the tiniest of dimples on her cheeks, Lin knew that he had lost his heart. As she arose and walked away, she averted her gaze and chastely covered her mouth with a fan. Lin could not take his eyes off her.

"Who is that woman," he wondered aloud.

"She is Sister Mei," the wizened woman at the temple gate told him with a knowing smirk. "Her name has spread far and wide, for she possesses a beauty that is not of this world."

On his way home that night, all Lin could think of was Sister Mei. He had been to the temple many times and there were always female devotees who would entice him into taking a second look. None were quite as beautiful as she was. Lin wondered what it would be like to have her hands entwined in his and to draw Sister Mei close to him, to hold her in his arms and gently place his lips upon hers.

When Lin reached home, he paused at the threshold. Everything had already been arranged for his journey. He had paid half the fare, and his belongings were packed. A trusted friend had agreed to watch over the house. All Lin had to do was go to the harbour in the morning, and he would be on his way.

But Lin knew that he had to see Sister Mei again. That night, he tossed and turned in bed for hours. When he finally drifted off to sleep, he dreamt of the beautiful woman at the temple. Sister Mei was standing in the moonlight at one of the temple courtyards, smiling coquettishly at him. For just an instant, Lin saw an old man with a red cord in his hand, standing in a corner and shaking his head in disapproval.

The very next day, Lin went to the temple again. He caught but a fleeting glimpse of Sister Mei before she retreated from his presence. Time and again, he took himself to the house of worship, with an offering here and a request to Mazu there. But he never saw Sister Mei for more than a few minutes. They did not exchange any words. She would offer her prayers, then give him the faintest of smiles before turning away. And yet, it felt as if he had been waiting for her his whole life. He had never imagined that it was possible to feel this way about a woman.

In his fervour, Lin did not consider that he knew nothing about the woman. It never occurred to Lin to wonder why she always wore the same tunic in the same shade of blue, or why a woman of noble stature, as she clearly was, was wandering around in a temple at all hours.

Lin's friends could see that all was not right. Why have you not set off on your journey, they asked. What is holding you back? He waved off their concerns. Lin had begun to lose weight. He often stayed awake through the night, and his general demeanor took on a dishevelled, slovenly look. He is bewitched, an old friend said, to the glum agreement of his peers. For Lin was no longer truly with them. He may as well have stepped onto that ship and sailed thousands of miles away.

Weeks passed. Or was it months? Then there came a moonlit evening when, at long last, he caught more than a glance of Sister Mei. She stopped in her tracks and waited for Lin beneath the masses of red lanterns that hung from the rooftop beams. Emboldened, he strode forward.

"Gong zi," she whispered in a voice that made him ache. How pale and fair she is, he thought. How lovely she is to look upon.

"Gu niang," he said as he bowed. "I am no gong zi. My family name is Lin." Ignoring the perplexing feelings inside of him and not caring if anyone saw, Lin took her hands in his. "You are lovelier than the brightest flowers of summer," he blurted out. "You are more beautiful than the sunrise."

Amid the stillness of the temple, Sister Mei beamed at Lin. The air was heavy with the aroma of candles and joss sticks that burned all around them. His heart racing, an understanding began to dawn upon him.

"Why," he asked, "are your hands so cold?"

Sister Mei was as still as the idols that lined the temple. But she did not speak.

Lin hesitated for just a moment. Whatever had seized him would not let go of him. "Will you," he asked haltingly. "Will you have me?"

"We cannot be together."

"Why?"

"We are not of the same world." A chill ran through Lin.

In the dim light of the temple, Sister Mei told her tale. "Once," she said, "I gave my life for someone I loved."

"My four sisters and I were concubines to a most noble

prince. He was a good man. He was a great man. He devoted himself to his people and to us."

Sister Mei sighed. "He had a voice like thunder. The officials of the court feared and respected him, as a mighty tiger that rules the forest. But to look into his eyes was to look upon the surface of a lake, placid and still. When the Prince took you into his arms, his touch was so gentle. It mattered not that he ultimately belonged to none of us. My sisters and I loved him more than anything else in this world."

"The day his forces lost the final battle with the Manchus, the prince decided that he no longer wished to live. He urged us to leave him, telling us that we were still young and had a future. Yuan, my eldest sister, was the first to cry. I will never forget her words. 'If the Prince lives, we all live. If the Prince dies, we all die.'"

Sister Mei's eyes glistened with tears. "I didn't want to die. I loved the Prince. But I loved life more."

"Why didn't you leave then?" asked Lin.

"All I had in the world were the Prince and my sisters. So I accepted the cord willingly. One by one, we hanged ourselves until breath left us, and our bodies turned cold."

There was a note of bitterness in her voice now. "But they didn't bury me with my sisters. In their haste to entomb us, they forgot about me. My body was left to the Manchus to defile. That is why I am still here."

The woman who had devoted her life to Zhu Shugui turned away from Lin. "I have been here, all by myself, for so very long. I have prayed to Mazu so many times to release me. But she does not answer. So many people come and go in the temple, but no one ever sees me. Except you."

Lin was neither frightened nor troubled by what he had heard. Instead, he took her hand and wiped her tears away tenderly. Sister Mei leaned into his hand and sighed. "You are just like the Prince."

Lin led her to the altar of Mazu, where they knelt before the deity. "Most Worthy and Efficacious Lady," intoned Lin. "Hear my prayer."

"All my life, I have sought virtue and honour. I treasure goodness and I despise evil. I have only ever sought to walk in the paths of righteousness, and to reject the ways of the wicked."

"But now," he said with a sharp intake of breath. "I will never be whole again if I am not with Sister Mei."

Lin inclined his head towards the impassive features of the divine lady, like a child pleading with its mother. "I know that the human and the spirit realms are as far apart as a man is from the day he left his mother's womb. I know that in Heaven's eyes, some things are not permitted."

The tears were welling up. "But I implore you, Ah Ma: let your divine hand be the bridge that brings us together. Now and forever, I want to be with Sister Mei." He turned towards the beautiful girl he loved. "If she will have me."

"For if we cannot be together in this world," he declared. "Then all that I wish for is to cross to the next one with her."

But Mazu did not appear as a pure beam of light or descend from heaven on a chariot of clouds, as some have claimed. Neither did the Divine Woman's emissaries Qianliyan and Shunfeng'er materialise to sweep them away. Instead, there was nothing more than a hush in the great temple, as the final echoes of Lin's prayer died away. The two lovers remained on bended knee before the altar, their hands interlocked, lost in each other.

From far off, a storm was coming. For the briefest moment, a flash of bright red robes could be seen in the thunder and the lightning.

A chill typically descends upon the listening crowd as the old woman ends her tale. It only takes half a minute or so for the question to be asked. "So what happened to them?"

"Ren you ren jian, gui you gui dao. Humans and ghosts belong in different worlds," the old woman will say solemnly. "The natural order of things must not be disrupted, for Heaven has decreed it so."

"But Mazu is not so hard-hearted," she adds. "For she is ever compassionate and merciful, and her great eye watches over all. If her favour shines upon you, anything is possible." In the grand tradition of storytellers everywhere, she bows with a flourish as the applause rings out. Then she walks away, always leaving the crowd wanting more.

It is said that every 10 years, on the 23rd day of the third lunar month, something unusual happens at the Grand Mazu Temple of Tainan, Taiwan. On that day, thousands of devotees come to celebrate the birthday of the goddess and to ask for a boon. If you are particularly pious, and your intentions are pure, and Mazu is pleased by your worship –

or so the story goes – it is said that the Divine Woman will grant you a most divine vision.

More than one person has seen it, but not everyone agrees on what they see. Some rejoice, while others are frightened out of their wits. Some are simply indifferent.

But most agree that it is a couple in what appears to be ancient clothes – she in a glistening blue tunic, he in scholarly attire – strolling side by side. He is smiling, she is covering her mouth chastely with a paper fan, and it appears as if they have all the time in the world. The couple can be seen only momentarily, before they fade away like the setting sun.

Heightened Alert

It was another impossibly blazing day in the remnants of the glorious utopia that was still called Singapore. Even with zombies roaming around in search of the next unfortunate meal, you could still count on only two kinds of weather in Singapore: hot and sticky, and wet and sticky. The end of the world wasn't enough: humanity had to be baked to death as well. It hadn't rained for almost a week now, and everyone who was still alive was going mad at a leisurely pace.

Sitting beneath the creaking ceiling fan in the four-room flat that had once been so prized, Lucas Wee could feel the sweat pouring from his brow, down his back and into his bermudas. Lucas wondered if zombies perspired. He hoped so. It was at least some small comfort to know that their existence might be as vexatious as that of the living.

He could see them across the car park from the windows of his third-floor flat, dozens of grey-skinned ghouls huddled in small groups at the void deck of the block opposite. It was all a bit of a blur, since Lucas couldn't see them clearly without his glasses, which he had made shortly before the start of the apocalypse for a hefty fee. It was the first pair of spectacles he had worn in his life, as his eyesight deteriorated in his 40s. But as befitted the end of days, he had dropped them in his rush to get away from the munchers, the day they ran full tilt at him.

He looked around the flat and took in the shattered fragments of his existence. Once upon a time, Lucas had been a neat freak, the kind who insisted that guests place their drinks on a coaster and carefully wiped away every stray bit of dirt. It was a habit inherited from his late parents, who had cleaned and tidied up so obsessively that food could have been eaten off the floor. Now, empty tins and cans were strewn everywhere, and the floor was sticky with grease and dirt. The flat reeked of decomposing leftovers and the sour odour of dried sweat. Even the rubbish chute was jammed shut now – any attempt to open it would have led to a torrent of garbage spilling out. For who was there left to clear the rubbish?

Lucas leaned back on his expensive leather sofa, cracked and grimy with sweat stains, and tried to remember what the world used to be like.

It had all started 28 days ago, with TikTok posts about a strange disease that left people feverish and gasping for air. Days after, they were writhing in their own blood and snot. Within weeks, they were hooked up to a respirator. Soon afterward, they left the vale of tears behind.

And then they found themselves hungry for something else.

Lucas could recall the exact moment that he first saw the news reports about the strange riots in the hospitals. He was scrolling through his Facebook feed while having bak chor mee and sipping an iced lemon tea at the kopitiam. The news had barely registered as he chomped down the rest of his meal. It turned out to be the last time he would ever eat there.

The first of the undead awoke in a packed ICU filled with frazzled healthcare workers, surrounded by the dying and the barely breathing. Within minutes, he got up and sank his teeth into the nearest nurse. Once that nurse revived, she got up and started biting others too. The running joke was that she had started with the most demanding of patients, followed by their annoying relatives. Or was it the ones in the B- and C-class wards? Regardless, the first swarm formed within hours and broke out of the hospital grounds, heading for the nearby MRT station.

There was barely even time to think about the surreal quality of the situation – zombies are real? – before things fell apart. The much-vaunted military with all its expensive toys turned out to be ineffectual. Half the NS boys had already been turned and the paper generals could not cope with anything that had not been played out on a laptop simulation. Public transport and other essential services shut down, and everyone retreated into their flats and condos and houses in short order. From that moment on, everything became a matter of survival.

Mercifully, water continued to flow from the taps, even when electricity became intermittent. Somehow, the internet still worked, which enabled the government to continue communicating with Singaporeans. The supermarkets and wet markets had closed long ago, so hundreds of secure pick-up points for food and everyday essentials had been established all over the island. These were regularly filled by immensely courageous logistics and military personnel, drawing from the country's emergency supplies. Lucas marvelled at the technological ingenuity that enabled entry to these points, which ranged from retrofitted bin centres to void deck storerooms to community centres, via Singpass. But whether you could actually reach them depended on a variety of factors.

First and foremost, you needed a functioning smartphone, laptop or tablet in order to access the link, sent out to millions via text message, to a map with the locations of these pick-up points. This was all assuming you actually possessed such a device and knew how to use it, which was far from guaranteed for the elderly, especially the ones who lived alone. If you were of the analogue persuasion, then you had to rely on maps in hard copy. The armed forces, as the organisation that still possessed the most manpower and resources, used helicopters to drop maps all over the island. It was not a bad idea in theory, but many were damaged or made illegible by the rain: some genius of a logistics officer had forgotten to waterproof the maps. Lucas couldn't imagine navigating his way around without Google Maps anyway. National Service, when they all had to make do with a map and compass, was a lifetime ago.

The next step was to figure where the nearest one was located, and how you were going to get there. There were now two things to consider: the buses and trains were no longer running, and masses of the formerly alive lay between you and the promised land.

In any case, how were you going to access the pick-up point if you didn't have a smartphone, let alone the Singpass app that would let you in? All of this meant that if you were old and lived alone and had trouble moving about, you were essentially fucked. But, like millions of other Singaporeans struggling to stay alive, this didn't particularly bother Lucas.

Lucas agonised over the thought of venturing to the nearest pick-up point, a good kilometre away. He shuddered at the prospect of running into a horde of munchers on the way there, or while on the way home with a heavy load of supplies. Like so many others afraid of stepping out of their homes, he was then reduced to scavenging from supermarkets, community gardens, rubbish bins and whatever could be found in the immediate vicinity. And yet, even the imminent dangers of the outside world did not prevent dozens from venturing far and wide. It wasn't just because they were compelled to look for food and drink: it was the sheer boredom of sitting at home with nothing to do. Perhaps it was the adrenaline from the fear that kept some alive.

The apocalypse was not restricted to Singapore. All over the world, the undead overran the major capitals and cities with no mercy. Civilisation fell apart as the remnants of humanity retreated into the mountains, or caves beneath the earth, or deserts where the infected could not survive the stultifying heat. The only downside to a functioning World Wide Web was that even the zombie apocalypse could not wipe out social media. Incredibly, there were still influencers posting videos of themselves weeping or dancing, sometimes simultaneously. Only cockroaches and influencers could survive the apocalypse, thought Lucas wryly.

Fake news refused to go away too. Some claimed that the virus was in the water that flowed from the taps, planted there by some secret cabal. Others claimed the munchers were nothing more than "zombies": paid actors in makeup, hired to provoke a global economic meltdown so that the oligarchs, Illuminati, or a random ethnic group could profit. It gave Lucas a great deal of satisfaction to see a particular influencer, who was known for her vicious trolling posts, filming herself attempting to confront the ghouls, only to be torn apart limb from limb. "Fake news! It's all fake news!" Her screams echoed, even as the infected tucked merrily into her torso and guts. Lucas had little else to do besides doomscrolling. It helped to take his mind off the hunger too.

But by far the most astounding posts Lucas came across were about what had become of the foreign worker dormitories. He had never been to one but knew from news reports that they were huge, with some as big as HDB estates. Some had been overrun by the undead, like so many other places in Singapore. But others had managed to hold out, the workers retreating behind the gates of their compound and setting up makeshift barricades to reinforce them. Supplied by air by the military, they had been instructed by the authorities not to leave, and dutifully, they obliged. For all intents and purposes, the dorms became self-sufficient townships.

Workers, if that was indeed who they were, posted videos of themselves cultivating their own vegetable plots and rearing chickens. They cooked, shared food, played badminton, laughed and joked around. In other words, they were living normal lives. Videos circulated of people attempting – and failing – to break into the dorms. Some even lambasted the government online, insisting that they be allowed into the dorms to take shelter.

The Cabinet had gone underground, with a Zombie Working Group – or the ZWG, as it insisted on calling itself with the civil service's strange love of acronyms – formed to continue the fight against the virus. Its scientists, hidden away in secret labs, were working with medical teams all over the world on a vaccine and a cure, though their progress was glacial.

The working theory was that the disease was airborne, so everyone was urged to wear surgical or cloth masks. This was transmitted to the populace via WhatsApp and Telegram video messages, while thousands of reusable masks were dropped by helicopter. "Please be socially responsible as you SFH," droned the bespectacled functionary whose face was beamed out each day alongside those of the co-chairs of the ZWG. "We can all Survive From Home if we look out for one another. We are not out of the woods, and will not be for a long time. We will continue to monitor the situation and take a step-by-step approach to the apocalypse."

Sometimes, they would trot out the Prime Minister, who looked increasingly wan and unwell, to reassure citizens in short video messages. Lucas was far from the only one who noticed that the PM sweated profusely through his zipped-up cardigan. He couldn't help wondering what those thick sleeves covered up. It reminded him of *The Kingdom*, the Korean drama series where the emperor had long ago turned into a zombie but was still dressed in his royal robes and made up to look human, while the scheming regent ruled in his place.

Everyone, including Lucas, kept to the advice of the ZWG religiously at first, until they realised that the government had one thing in common with ordinary citizens, in that the sum total of their knowledge about the virus amounted to the same as theirs: not a lot. Messages from the authorities quickly degenerated into a slew of naggy, pointless reminders. They even advised you not to drink alcohol after 10.30 at night, apparently because it would increase your body heat and attract the munchers, who were generally more active after last light. Lucas pictured them lying in wait in the bushes, all staring at their watches until the clock struck 10.30. He sniggered out loud at this.

There was also the head-scratching instruction to carry a tape measure around in order to maintain a distance of at least one metre from the undead, so that you would be safe from infection. What Lucas found even stranger was that some actually heeded this advice. Once, while he was out scrounging for supplies, he stumbled upon a masked uncle being taken down by a group of munchers, measuring tape in hand. The man's final words still rang in his head, "But it's one metre! I was one metre apart!" Lucas responded by turning tail and ensuring that he kept a distance of several hundred metres from the uncle.

Certain ironclad rules still applied. You never went out alone at night. You always brought a backpack along to store whatever food or supplies you could find. You never ventured too far from home, and you always carried some kind of weapon. For Lucas, it was a sturdy wooden leg taken from one of his dining chairs, which had fallen apart. He had yet to find out how effective it was against the undead.

But they were an unpredictable lot, and this was exacerbated by the weather. The heat seemed to drain their energy, just like for normal human beings. Most of the time, they shuffled around harmlessly in a trance, unless you were foolish enough to attract their attention. But all bets were off when the rain came lashing down, which always occurred with little warning. It supercharged the infected, and they went after every living thing, even stray dogs and cats, as one wild, frenzied swarm. That was when you ran for your life and didn't look back.

Lucas had not washed himself or changed his clothes for three days now. He spent most of his time lying in bed or on the kitchen floor, or as far from the front door as he could humanly manage. He clenched his jaw as he thought about the last time he had opened it.

Returning to his corner unit that day, Lucas unlocked the grille gate and the door before stumbling into his flat. He dumped his stained and filthy backpack on the floor, along with the wooden chair leg, and let out a deep breath. He sat on the floor, his head clutched in his hands, and shut his eyes.

The hurried trip to the nearby supermarket, long abandoned and looted a dozen times over, had yielded just a few bottles of fizzy, sugary drinks and three bloated cans of expired spam. He had hurriedly dumped them in his backpack and run off as quickly as he could. Lucas knew it was only a matter of time before the supermarket was completely emptied and the hunger set in. That would leave him no choice but to head to the pick-up point. Who knew how many of the infected he would have to negotiate along the way, or what the weather might be like? After all these, there were no more weather forecasts to consult.

Lucas sometimes felt like the main character in a zombie apocalypse movie. And of all the tired old tropes of the genre – the survivors huddled around the campfire, the hard-nosed survivor hiding a terrible secret – he had been stuck with the worst one of all: the lone protagonist. In the many, many hours that he had spent contemplating his existence, his late mother's gentle admonishment constantly came to mind, "It's not good to be alone all the time, Lucas."

After his parents passed, he had gotten too used to the solitude, isolating himself from family and friends and becoming uncomfortable with close relationships. Even at work, he kept things cordial but cool. Now, at the end of the world, just when he most needed it, there was no one left to ask for help. The neighbours on his floor had all died or fled, while the others in his block were ensconced in their flats and rarely came out. He tried texting some friends he had not contacted in years, but no one responded.

It was the ding of the elevator, just a little way down the corridor, and the whir of the doors opening that jolted Lucas to his senses. His body tensing, he knew what was there even before he turned around.

It was an old lady, dressed in a grey blouse and black pants, who emerged shambling and snarling from the lift.

Her complexion was a dark shade of grey, and her arms dangled by her side. She sniffed the air and lurched forward with a limp. In life, she might have spent her days chatting with friends at the void deck, and beaming at the children in the playground. Now, she turned sharply to her left and saw Lucas. Emitting a high-pitched groan, she lurched forward. That was when Lucas belatedly realised that he had forgotten to close both gate and door.

He slammed the gate shut and fumbled with his keys as he desperately tried to lock it. The lift could not have been more than 10 metres away, and the ah ma was rapidly closing the distance, her banshee-like wails ringing in his ears. Can zombies open doors, he thought, as he lost all sense of hand-eye coordination. It was the worst possible time to find out.

He cursed as he dropped his keys. She was just three or four steps away.

Lucas had not known that he was capable of moving at such speed. Crouching, he grabbed the chair leg with both hands and in the same motion, sprang up and jammed it through the gaps in the gate, just in time to meet the elderly zombie's forehead. She froze for a moment before collapsing. Her blackened arms, which had been thrust through the grille gate, now rested half on the threshold, half on the living room floor. She lay face down on the steps before the flat, as if kowtowing in supplication to a distant deity.

Lucas gingerly pushed her arms through the gap with his feet. He picked up his keys and locked the grille gate, before slamming the door shut and locking that in turn. Then he lay down in a foetal position and dry heaved and cried, all at the same time.

Lucas snapped out of his reverie and back into the present. He could see his battered backpack from the corner of his eye. It sat by the door, salt trails from his sweat all over it, just waiting to be used.

He took out his phone and clicked on the link in his WhatsApp messages again. He did a search based on postal codes, and found the pick-up point nearest to home: a run-down bin centre, alongside a map with precise directions. Though he had long ago committed the straightforward route to memory, he studied the map for the hundredth time. "It takes about 20 minutes to get to the pick-up point, if I move fast," he said out loud. "Maybe another 15 minutes to pack up the stuff, after that, 20 more to come back home." Lucas had taken to talking to himself to fill the silence.

"Provided I don't die on the way there. Or back."

The link also came with photos of the pack of provisions, sufficient for seven days, to which each person was entitled. It included biscuits, instant noodles and rice, canned meat, chocolate and packets of powdered drinks. They were all sealed within large dark green packets, like the kind he used to get in the army. It made Lucas salivate just to look at the image. The last thing he had eaten was an expired can of sardines, and that was three days ago. Despite the pangs in his stomach, he had decided against opening the bloated cans of spam.

In normal times, bin centres served as storage spaces for rubbish bins and sometimes as a sleeping or living space for foreign workers. They were typically small, one-storey buildings, tucked away in some nondescript corner of a

HDB estate. Since they were equipped with roller shutters, someone had realised that they made for ideal pick-up points, being easily secured and accessible.

Lucas glanced at his watch, and looked over to the living room windows, where the harsh sunlight streamed through. There were plenty of hours left before dusk, and the weather looked good. But Lucas was paralysed. "Get the fuck up and move," he hissed, as if he were telling off the students he had once taught. Lucas sprang to his feet, only to sit back down immediately. He was dizzy with hunger.

He reached for his water bottle and sucked down the remainder of its contents. When a few minutes had passed, he got up again, slowly this time, and went to retrieve his backpack. Picking up the chair leg, Lucas tucked it into the bag and zipped it up. Just enough of it was exposed so that he could easily pull it out if he needed to.

Standing before the door, Lucas unlocked it and clenched his eyes shut. He opened them and swung the door wide open to be assaulted by the sight and smell of the ah ma. He choked. Her face was covered with buzzing flies and maggots, and the odour that emanated from her was abominable. Gritting his teeth, Lucas unlocked the gate and jumped over the corpse. Slamming the door of his unit shut, Lucas locked up and turned his attention to the cadaver.

"Sorry, Ah Ma." Grimacing, he grabbed both of her blackened forearms and heaved. The flies, interrupted in their feasting, immediately swarmed around him. He looked away, trying not to acknowledge the wet trail of writhing maggots and bodily fluids he left in his wake. He got as far as five metres before one of her wrists came off. Lucas yelled in shock as he flung the detached appendage over the parapet of the corridor. Grabbing the other wrist and what remained of the old woman's forearm, he continued pulling, gingerly this time, until he got to the staircase. Clenching his teeth, he manoeuvred the body into position and used his foot to tip it down the stairs. As it rolled forward, it disintegrated into several pulpy pieces, leaving the flies even angrier than before. It all landed with a wet splash.

Lucas looked at his hands, which were stained black with unknown fluids. Wiping them furiously on the walls, he proceeded to fly down the stairs, his hunger forgotten. He jumped over the shattered remains of the old woman and flew down three flights to the ground floor. The elevator still worked, but he had been having nightmares about being in the lift, only to have the door open and reveal a swarm of zombies waiting for him. It felt safer to be on foot.

Advancing from the lift lobby, Lucas stepped out from under shelter and into the sunlight. It was the stench that hit him first, and he gagged involuntarily. He squinted, and as his eyes adjusted to the light, he gasped. He had not paid much attention to the large grass field, once the venue for innumerable getai performances, which lay before his block and separated it from the car park. Dozens of bodies littered the overgrown grass. Many of them were children.

Lucas fought off the urge to vomit – there was nothing in his stomach to throw up anyway – and swiftly moved on from the field. He reached the car park, which was still filled with cars and motorbikes. Lucas slowed down at the sight of the grey horde at the block opposite. A low snarling emanated from them, like a pack of wolves, as they ambled around aimlessly just a few metres from him. "Turn right, go straight, then go down the staircase and cross the first traffic lights. Don't go too fast," he whispered to himself. Lucas broke into a brisk jog, taking care not to move too quickly so as not to attract the munchers. He once made the mistake of sprinting past a mob of them, which had the opposite effect of getting their attention instead. He had barely gotten away from them then.

He scanned everything in front of him as he moved forward, his eyes looking left and right for unseen munchers. Every abandoned vehicle felt like a potential ambush or death trap. He was the only person in the car park, but felt certain that there were residents overhead watching him. The sweat was already pouring down his brow and neck. But Lucas was making good progress. It was almost time to cut into the nearest void deck, before going down any of a number of staircases to the pavement, and on to the traffic lights. From there, it was a straight jog all the way to the pick-up point. If he didn't know any better, Lucas could have been on a leisurely stroll to the market for afternoon tea.

Lucas inhaled deeply. There was a familiar scent in the air that reminded him of better times. It brought back a memory of a word he had heard long ago: petrichor. The tension gradually went out of his body and he slowed his pace. In his head, a fantasy took shape of what he might eat at the market. He had always liked what the chwee kueh stall served up, with plenty of chilli to go with the preserved radish topping atop the steamed rice cakes. Lucas might also order an iced kopi C siu dai and find a seat on the edge of the market, away from the stuffy centre. He always enjoyed sitting there with a book and reading for a few hours, whiling away the time.

The scene in his mind was so pleasing that Lucas didn't even notice that the sun had gone down. The light had turned dusky, and the scent in the air was almost overpowering. With mounting horror, he remembered what petrichor meant: the earthy smell that comes when rain falls on the earth.

Lucas froze in his tracks when he felt the first raindrop on his cheek. He looked up, and another fell on his forehead. And then another. He looked behind him. The grey horde, still shuffling around aimlessly, were tiny figures in the not-too-far distance. With a clap of thunder, the heavens opened and the rain came pouring down. Ignoring the churning feeling in his stomach, Lucas took off. Behind him came the familiar collective wail of the infected, followed by the rumble of pounding footsteps as they spotted him and gave chase.

He did not dare look back but knew exactly what had happened. As the rain fell, the undead would perk up, like a dog smelling a treat, and sniff the air cautiously at first. Then they would all start snarling, wolves getting ready to hunt. Once the pack spotted their prey, the pursuit began. As Lucas sprinted for his life, he could hear the cries of residents above him. "Zao ah, zao ah!"

Furiously wiping the rain out of his eyes, Lucas made it down the staircase to the pavement and ran for the traffic lights. His legs and lungs burning, he could see the bin centre nearing as he crossed the road. It was barely a hundred metres away. Gasping for air, he caught his second wind and picked up the pace. Lucas could hear the wails of the undead behind him, closing in inexorably. Lucas pulled out his phone and tapped on the Singpass app. He stared at it and let it load as it read his face. The QR code reader, which lay perched atop a tall pole at chest level like a parking meter in front of the bin centre, was now within touching distance.

Lucas came to an abrupt halt. His chest heaving up and down, he took a moment to steady himself before pointing his phone at the reader. With a click and a whir, the roller shutters that secured the bin centre began ascending gradually. The infected were slipping and sliding in the rain. They would reach him in a matter of seconds.

Once the shutters had reached his knees, Lucas crouched and rolled himself into the bin centre. Activated by motion sensors, the lights and the oscillating fans within came to life, lighting up the interior. Jumping up, he frantically wiped the moisture from his phone and pointed it at the corresponding code reader inside the tiny building. With a shudder, the shutters slowly, slowly reversed course. They touched down just as the first of the munchers reached the bin centre and slammed into the shutters, causing Lucas to jump back. These were followed by multiple crashes as the wailing, snarling throng outside laid siege to the pick-up point. But the shutters held firm.

Lucas looked around him. There were a dozen massive vending machines, each one secured behind a thin cage, with a gap near the bottom to dispense its contents. There were different labels for each one like CANNED FOOD and TOILETRIES and CUP NOODLES. They were packed with bottled drinks like green tea and 100 Plus, as well as detergent and even toothbrushes. He went straight for the machine labelled PROVISION PACK. Lucas scanned his Singpass app and a pack fell onto the floor through the gap. Ripping it open, he took out a packet of biscuits and tore that open. He popped one in his mouth and slowly savoured it. Lucas sighed. It would do for now.

There was a faint odour of chlorine in the air. As he munched one biscuit after another, he read the leaflet inside the pack. It consisted of a series of instructions and reminders such as "Please do not take more supplies than you need" and "The pick-up point is replenished every three days. The national stockpile is more than sufficient and the government will ensure that all Singaporeans have enough to eat."

Then he came to the header: "What to do if you find yourself trapped at the pick-up point".

"Do not panic," it began. "The shutters are strong enough to keep out the infected. Stay away from the entrance, so that they cannot smell you. The infected will eventually move on. We recommend that you leave the following morning at first light for your own safety.

"Do not stay in the pick-up point unless absolutely necessary. This is not a living space and is needed for storage of essential supplies. We will remove you if need be. Military and government personnel are armed and have discretion to determine if you are a threat."

Lucas looked at his watch. Barely 45 minutes had passed since he left his flat. Now that the adrenaline had worn off, the fatigue was setting in. He felt like a balloon that was slowly deflating.

He took out his phone and saw the notification for the daily WhatsApp message sent out by the ZWG. There wasn't likely to be any new information besides the habitual reminders, but Lucas clicked on it anyway. It was a video, starring the bespectacled man once again. He appeared to be sitting in some sort of bunker. He looked comfortable and well-fed.

"Good morning, fellow Singaporeans," he said. "It is Day 28 of the apocalypse. Singapore is still here. Your government is still working for you. And we will get through this together, if we each play our part. Please remember to be socially responsible as you SFH, and know that we are here for you."

Lucas laughed hysterically. He couldn't wait to survive from home.

Mr Kim

The first time Mr Kim walked into the parlour, Jimmy thought he was an extremely successful hawker. With his meaty, powerful arms, the man would have looked right at home chopping up chicken at a stall, or stir frying Hokkien prawn mee. In another life, Mr Kim might have been the kind of towkay so beloved of the Chinese tabloids – the ones that drove BMWs, wore gold chains, kept a mistress or two, and eventually ended up in court for tax evasion.

He was a rotund, middle-aged man with very little hair, who wore round-rimmed spectacles and a messy smattering of stubble on his jawline. A gold ring sat on his left pinkie and his baggy, ill-matched designer clothes looked as if they had been haphazardly swiped off the rack. His paunch hung comfortably over his belt, and the stench of cigar smoke hung over him like a cloud. If Mr Kim had lived in the 1980s, he would have carried one of the first-generation mobile phones, the ones that were as long as a brick and about as heavy.

The first clue that Mr Kim might be more than he appeared was the sizeable entourage that accompanied him, who made the wind chimes above the doors tinkle continuously as they made their entrance in quick succession. There were four men with severe buzzcuts, dressed in dark suits and glaring at everyone murderously. Despite the oppressive weather, Jimmy never saw them take off the jackets or loosen their ties. Each of them had a bulge beneath their clothes that made him think of the sidearms and earpieces of FBI agents in the movies.

Then there were the women. They were a quartet, each with hair coloured in different shades of brown or silver. They looked to be in their 30s and were clearly hungover. One of them even had tiny traces of white powder on her nose, and she kept sniffling as if she had a cold. They were almost identical – slim, leggy, buxom women in short, dark-coloured skirts and buttoned-up blouses. They look like a low-budget K-pop girl group, thought Jimmy as they staggered in, daintily dabbing the sweat off their foreheads. He recognised the lyrical sounds of the Korean language as they conversed, thanks to the insufferable Korean dramas his wife forced him to sit through.

Wiping the sweat off his brow with a silk handkerchief, Mr Kim strode casually towards the counter where Jimmy sat behind a cash register. Jimmy couldn't help wondering if the parlour was about to get robbed.

"Good afternoon. You are the tattoo artist?" Mr Kim spoke in light tones, with only a faint trace of a Korean accent.

Jimmy cleared his throat and tried his best to look professional. "Yes, I'm Jimmy. Do you have an appointment, Mr …?"

"Kim. Call me Henry. We have no appointment." He looked over his shoulder at the ladies behind him and smiled thinly. "My friends would like tattoos."

"Nice to meet you, Mr Kim. But we don't really do walk-ins. We have a lot of clients today as well. Do you want to come back another day?"

"I apologise for not calling ahead, Mr Jimmy. I am only in town for a few days and I have a very busy schedule." He gestured to one of the men in suits, who stepped forward with a slight bow, reached behind him and pulled the thick money pouch around his waist to the front. Jimmy maintained a deadpan expression as the man unzipped the pouch to reveal a thick wad of notes, neatly placed in different compartments. Though he only caught a glimpse, Jimmy recognised the telltale colours of US dollar and British pound notes, among a myriad of other currencies. It all easily amounted to tens of thousands of dollars. Does he think this is a drug deal, wondered Jimmy.

"We will pay a good price, of course," said Mr Kim. More than a few clients had in the past barged into the parlour, flashing the cash and demanding this or that design. Some were in tears or drunk, sometimes both, like the man who wanted a tattoo of his wife's name and IC number on his forearm. While they clearly had not thought things through, Jimmy didn't see himself as the moral police. It was not his job to advise them to give their requests more thought. Whether he and his colleagues acceded to their requests depended on three things: his mood, the customer's mood — one of them had smashed up the parlour in a drunken rage and the police had to be called – and above all, whether it was an interesting design.

"It's not about the money. We can't fit another four more people today."

Mr Kim reached into his breast pocket and took out a folded piece of paper, placing it on the counter. The light glinted off his Rolex as he withdrew his hand.

"We would like this design."

Jimmy unfolded the paper. It was a black-and-white drawing of a tiger, crouched as if ready to pounce, teeth bared and tail coiled in the air. Its bulging eyes had a savage fury in them. The drawing was so intricately rendered that he could almost feel the tiger's fur bristling. It was gorgeous.

He looked up to find Mr Kim waiting patiently with that same thin smile, his hands clasped before him. Jimmy looked at the tiger design again and had a think. He tapped on the tablet before him, propped upright on its stand, and consulted a schedule on an Excel sheet. It was doable.

"How about this – we can do this design today, but for only two of the ladies. We will work on the other two if they come back tomorrow. Can?"

"Yes, that is acceptable."

"Also, since you don't have an appointment and we need to change our schedule, we will charge 25% more."

"No problem at all." Mr Kim did not bother enquiring about the actual price.

"All right. Where do your friends want it?"

"On the chest, just above the bosom."

"I see. Please give me a minute." He got up and stepped through a red curtain into the work area. Inside, there was a series of leather-clad foldable beds, each separated by more curtains, and all occupied by customers. Whether the curtains were drawn depended on which part of the body the artists were working on, and the clients' comfort levels.

"Becky, Sandy! Can I talk to you?"

Two women in black gloves put down their tattoo pens and walked over to Jimmy, who was standing at the curtain. Rubbing their necks and shoulders, they looked at him expectantly.

"I got lobang for you all. Want not?"

"I'm just about to finish one client leh. And there's another one coming at six," said Becky. She moved gingerly, as she was still feeling the effects of the slipped disc she had sustained while working on a client six months before. Her hands seized up at times as well, but she remained one of the best tattooists at Jimmy's collective.

"Me too," added Sandy. Like most of the artists working at Jimmy's parlour, she favoured body art featuring animals. She had a pair of kittens on the inside of her wrist, while Becky had one of her late dog on her thigh.

"Check this out," said Jimmy in a low voice as he drew back the curtain ever so slightly to show them the waiting area. "It's for the women over there." Jimmy showed them the tiger design and they were instantly transfixed. But the doubt remained in their eyes.

"We'll do two of them today, and another two tomorrow. I'm charging them 25% more, so your fee will also increase by a quarter. I looked at the schedule – you both have no clients for the next two days, so you can take a long break after this."

Jimmy added, "These people have money to spend. I think they will come back one. So let's accommodate them."

Becky and Sandy nodded.

"OK, come with me." Jimmy gestured them over. They stepped into the waiting area.

"Mr Kim, my colleagues here will take care of your friends," said Jimmy.

"You're not going to do it yourself, Mr Jimmy?"

"Since it's an intimate area, I think it would be better for a lady to do it."

Mr Kim flashed that smile again. He barked an order at the women, and two of them followed the tattoo artists beyond the red curtain. That left Jimmy with Mr Kim and the rest of his entourage, locked in an awkward silence in the waiting area.

"How long will it take?"

"It depends. It's quite a detailed design, so maybe two or three hours?"

"I shall take a walk then," said Mr Kim. He exited the parlour, followed closely by the men in suits and the remaining women. Once they were out of sight, Jimmy exhaled loudly in bemusement. He wryly wondered if Mr Kim's men might pull out shotguns and shoot up the whole place if the tattoos weren't up to scratch.

Several hours later, the women emerged from the work area, the transparent skin plasters on their chests only partially covered by their blouses, and took seats in the waiting area. Right on cue, Mr Kim and his minions returned shortly after. The women immediately jumped up, and walked over to Mr Kim. He gestured, and they unbuttoned their tops to show him the artists' handiwork. The boss looked them over for a full minute.

Turning to Jimmy, Mr Kim declared, "This is excellent work, Mr Jimmy. Please tell your artists that they have done very well."

"Thank you, Mr Kim. I'm glad you like it." And I hope your friends like it too, thought Jimmy. He was fairly certain the women did not have a say in the matter.

Mr Kim nodded, and the man with the money pouch stepped forward. Pulling out the pouch, he placed several thousand-dollar notes on the counter. "Payment. All," said the man gruffly. He also pulled Jimmy's name card from the stack on the counter and placed it in his inner coat pocket.

"But this is too much," protested Jimmy.

"Do not worry, Mr Jimmy," said Mr Kim. "This is payment for tomorrow as well. For the excellent work." Before Jimmy could respond, he swept out of the parlour, his entourage of mysterious women and scary men trailing him.

The next day came and went with little incident. The remaining two women returned the following day, accompanied by just one of the men in suits. Since none of them spoke English, they communicated via gestures and Google Translate. Once the artwork was done, the flunkey got the women to take off their tees and took photos of the finished tattoo with just a little too much enthusiasm. Jimmy would have asked them not to do that in the waiting area, but he was afraid the man might murder him. The Korean then tapped on his phone several times and waited. His phone lit up a minute later. The besuited man glanced briefly at the screen, flashed a thumbs-up at Jimmy and ushered the women out the door.

Mr Kim would visit the parlour twice more in the course of that year. The second time, he turned up unannounced again, accompanied by a different group of women in matching outfits. Once more, he had a specific, intricate design, this time of a pair of butterflies, to be rendered at an intimate part of the body. Becky and Sandy did the job again, and once more, Mr Kim praised their handiwork. And of course, he overpaid again. But as far as Jimmy was concerned, Mr Kim could pay any amount he wanted, as long as his artists were not shortchanged.

The third time, he surprised Jimmy by mailing ahead. The email with the header "Can you do this for me, Mr Jimmy?", sent by a Henry Kim, popped up on the tablet one afternoon. It consisted of the words "right side of chest", together with a date and time, and an attachment. Jimmy opened it to find another beautiful black-and-white design, this time of a somewhat cartoonish bat in flight, its teeth bared and its pupils tiny dots.

It was a no-brainer. Jimmy replied in the affirmative, together with his quote. Mr Kim's response was equally swift: "See you on Friday."

Mr Kim turned up on the dot, plugged into his earphones and dressed in a Hawaiian shirt and slacks with socks and sandals. He was accompanied by one of the heavies, who carried a paper bag. Jimmy recognised him as the most severe-looking of the lot. He resembled a scriptwriter's depiction of a gangster, with a long diagonal scar running from his eyebrow, down his nose and onto his right cheek.

All he needed was to get into a fight where his clothes got torn off to reveal dragon tattoos on his chest, and he would be the complete walking cliché.

"Please follow me, Mr Kim," said Jimmy, gesturing to the red curtain. He wasn't usually this formal with clients, but he found himself subconsciously aping the behaviour of Mr Kim's minions.

Mr Kim waved off the bodyguard, who was about to accompany him into the work area and had begun to protest when the boss cut him off sharply. Suitably chastened, he took a seat in the waiting area.

Once inside the work area, Mr Kim took his shirt off to reveal a tattoo of a samurai warrior reeling in two carps, which covered the entirety of his stomach. His biceps were covered with dragon and koi designs as well. Jimmy couldn't help but admire the artwork as the Korean hung the shirt on a nearby hook. He pulled out his earphones, exposing the soft strains of Eric Clapton's "Layla", before coiling and putting them in his trouser pocket. Finally, he lay down on one of the beds.

Jimmy stifled a grin. In that moment, he resembled a rather large, but harmless, bear.

Putting on his spectacles, Jimmy sat on a stool beside the bed and adjusted the height. Then he pulled on gloves and opened a fresh package of cartridge needles. He inserted one into the tattoo pen before putting it aside on a tray with the rest of his implements. He focused first on cleaning the target area of Mr Kim's chest with antiseptic.

"I don't think I ever asked you. How did you find out about our parlour?"

"I saw you on Instagram. You came highly recommended too."

"That's nice to hear." A part of Jimmy knew it was wisest to know as little as possible about the Korean. Still, he couldn't help asking the question.

"What do you do, Mr Kim?" Despite his amiable nature, Jimmy couldn't help addressing him formally.

"I am a businessman."

A businessman who travels with four security guards, stacks of cash and his personal harem, thought Jimmy. "What kind of business?"

"I run gaming websites."

"That must be good money." Once he was done with the antiseptic, Jimmy applied the stencil solution to Mr Kim's chest. He then proceeded to carefully place the transfer paper with the design on it, rubbing it down with a paper towel.

"Yes. You can always count on the punters," he replied with a chuckle.

"Was that always your aspiration?"

"No. I started this because I needed to get away from the family business."

"Your father wanted you to take over, I guess?"

"Yes, at first. But in the end, he favoured my younger brother."

Jimmy nodded in sympathy. In Korean dramas there were always stories involving chaebol, or family-controlled conglomerates. It didn't take an intimate knowledge of Korean culture to imagine the sorts of pressures that the scions are subject to.

"What is the family business? If you don't mind my asking."

"All kinds of things. Logistics. Food and beverage. Human resource. And so on."

"I guess your brother runs it now?"

"Yes, he does," said Mr Kim. "I had to leave because he saw me as a threat, after our father died. In the end, I left Korea altogether."

"I see." They had a couple of minutes more before the stencil solution dried. "Are you happier now, doing this business?"

"Le coeur a ses raisons que la raison ignore."

"What's that?"

"The heart has reasons that reason cannot know."

Jimmy nodded as if he understood. He had heard more than enough dime store philosophy from clients. Some rambled on in a stupor, while others spoke clear as day.

"Where did you get your tattoo designs from, Mr Kim?"

"I draw them myself." He gestured with his chin towards the tattoo on Jimmy's neck. "I like your fox."

"Thank you. So you're an artist too?"

"In my younger days, I wanted to be one. My auntie said I was hot-tempered and sensitive, and gifted in the arts. But my father disapproved."

"Your father sounds very strict."

His next words sent a chill through Jimmy. "When I was a child, he chained me to the toilet and beat me. He told me it would make me strong."

After more than a decade in the business, Jimmy was used to being told the most intimate secrets. There was the woman with the hyper-religious parents who didn't allow her to wear shorts or skirts, as well as the man who had grown up in a cult where his entire extended family were members. Some stories, like that of the couple who got matching tattoos of their autistic son who had died suddenly, were so desperately sad that Jimmy had no words in response. It was as if his clients had stepped into a confessional booth. But though he was always sympathetic, Jimmy pushed his emotions aside, for all he truly cared about was rendering a great design.

"My father was strangely contradictory," continued Mr Kim, as if he were recalling what he had had for breakfast. "He would beat me mercilessly. At other times, he sent his men all over the world to buy me gifts. Once, he gave me a gold-plated toy gun. I treasured it for a very long time."

He took a long pause. "But I did not want his gifts. All I truly wanted was his love. In the end, he decided that he loved my younger brother most."

"I'm very sorry to hear that."

"There is nothing to be sorry about, Mr Jimmy."

He glanced at his watch. "Shall we begin, Mr Kim?"

"Yes, please."

Jimmy peeled off the transfer paper, leaving the outline of the tattoo on Mr Kim's chest. With a hard copy of the bat design for reference, he picked up the tattoo pen and switched it on. Amid the continued low din of the buzzing machine, the tattoo gradually took shape for the next two hours.

The work proceeded largely in silence. Mr Kim lapsed into deep thought, while Jimmy focused on the design, carefully pricking and dabbing and wiping. It was Mr Kim who spoke first.

"Are those swallows on your arm, Mr Jimmy?"

"Yes, my first tattoo."

"What do they symbolise?"

"Safe travels. Sailors used to get tattoos of swallows because it meant that land was near, and they would get home safely."

"I wonder if I will ever see home again."

"You don't intend to go home?"

"It is not safe for me. Or my children."

Jimmy wasn't certain whether he ought to ask the question or not. But he did it anyway. "Because of your brother?"

Mr Kim nodded. "I have tried to tell him that I have no interest in the family business. He does not believe me." He pondered his next words for a moment. "I am afraid he may do something foolish."

"Foolish?"

"I am afraid for my life."

"Well, surely he won't harm his own brother." With his bodyguards and rotating roster of women and bags of cash, Mr Kim certainly looked the part of a gangster. But Jimmy didn't know if he was the real deal, or simply a rich man's son indulging a fantasy. Nevertheless, it didn't hurt to play along with him.

"Half-brother. My father had many women."

"Blood is still thicker than water, no?" The bat was taking shape, its fangs bared and its leathery wings outstretched.

"When you want something badly enough, Mr Jimmy, even blood will not stop you." Jimmy had no response to that. So he continued working on the bat.

Forty-five minutes later, Jimmy was done. Laying his tools aside, he admired his handiwork for just a bit before picking up a mirror and showing it to the Korean. Mr Kim gazed into it. He beamed.

"Thank you, Mr Jimmy. It is very beautiful."

"You're welcome, Mr Kim. Glad you like it." He applied the skin plaster. "I think you know the drill. Keep it dry for the next few days. No swimming for at least a week. Apply moisturiser."

"I know the drill indeed." He dismounted the bed and got dressed.

As they walked into the waiting area, Mr Kim's flunkey got up at once. With a little bow, he proffered the paper bag to Jimmy.

"For all your excellent work," said Mr Kim.

"Thank you." Jimmy knew it was pointless to protest. Stealing a glance inside, he saw a large note and what appeared to be a very fancy and very expensive bottle of soju. There was no need to check the amount.

"Goodbye, Artist Jimmy," he said with an elaborate bow. "I will be back in Singapore next year. Perhaps I will bring more friends here."

Turning on his heel, Mr Kim walked out the door, trailed closely by his faithful manservant. As the sounds of the chimes faded, Jimmy had a feeling that he would never see him again.

He was right.

Jimmy yawned. He had just finished a marathon session in the morning, putting the finishing touches to a family portrait that covered a man's entire back. He had lost his wife and two children in an accident two years before, and wanted to memorialise them. "I want them to be with me forever," he said with a glassy-eyed stare.

It had taken two sessions to finish it, and felt more like a therapy session, with extended periods of sobbing. Jimmy felt for the man and had taken extra care to get the details right. At the end of it, when he saw the end result, he hugged Jimmy and wept on his shoulder.

Sitting at the counter, Jimmy lazily flicked through his Instagram feed on his tablet, tapping on random videos. He wasn't really paying attention. All he wanted was some background noise.

Jimmy tapped on a news video and fast forwarded past the introduction. "... shocking news out of the Malaysian capital today, of a daring assassination carried out in broad daylight at Kuala Lumpur International Airport."

Since when is news not shocking, he thought, stifling a yawn. Propping up his elbow on the counter, he rested his chin on his hand and zoned out. As Jimmy closed his eyes, he only caught snatches of the broadcast.

"Much of KLIA has been shut down ... two women arrested ... one Vietnamese, one Indonesian ...a claimed they thought they were taking part in a televised prank ... apparent use of the nerve agent VX ... causes confusion, chest tightness, difficulty breathing ... the number one suspect: North Korean leader Kim Jong Un."

It was the newscaster's next words that made Jimmy sit up straight and pay attention. "The first-born son of the late Kim Jong Il, and half-brother to the present leader of North Korea, Kim Jong Nam was just 45 years old. While he has not been officially identified, police are almost certain it is him, thanks to his distinctive tattoos."

A photo of the deceased flashed on the screen. Jimmy froze. He stared at the image before him and blinked slowly. Then he rewound the video and scrutinised that roly-poly visage with the round-rimmed glasses and the smattering of stubble again.

There was no mistaking that amiable manner and the barely visible smile.

The sounds of the news broadcast faded into the background, as Jimmy sat motionless on his stool. Even when Becky came by and asked what he wanted for lunch, he did not respond. Everything started to add up now.

Jimmy jumped a little when Becky stepped out of the parlour, setting off the wind chimes once again. All he could think about were Mr Kim's words.

When you want something badly enough, even blood will not stop you.

Acknowledgements

Thanks be to God Almighty, for His guidance, inspiration and protection.

This book would not have been possible without the help of all those who told me their tales. You have my eternal gratitude, and I hope that I have done your stories justice.

With much thanks to my editor She-reen Wong, for her always forthright feedback and invaluable ideas, and for checking my more long-winded tendencies.

I am immensely grateful for the feedback and suggestions of Kelly Ng, Wong Pei Ting, Evelyn Fong, Noorul Raaha As'art and Maisarah Abu Samah.

Much thanks to my Mother and Second Aunt, who racked their brains for memories of the past and put up with my endless queries about my grandmother.

Special thanks to Grace Moon and Ahn Ye Hoon for sharing their thoughts and suggestions on *The Woodcutter*. I also leaned greatly on *Korean Folk And Fairy Tales* by Suzanne Crowder Han. The research of Dr David Palmer of the University of Melbourne on Korean forced labourers during World War II as well as the accounts of these labourers

Acknowledgements

in the late Eidai Hiyashi's *Forced Into Forced Labour;* were very helpful too.

With thanks to Julian for generously sharing his thoughts and experiences as a tattoo artist for *Mr Kim*. *The Great Successor* by Anna Fifield was also immensely enlightening, as was the reporting of media outlets such as Reuters, *The Wall Street Journal* and *The New Straits Times*.

The sources for *The Queen of Heaven* remain, among others, the writings of Jonathan Winthrope, Riley Winters, Lin Yaoyu and Lin Linchang. *The Dream Hunters* by Neil Gaiman and Yoshitaka Amano is a key influence, as well as the classic movie *A Chinese Ghost Story*.

About the Author

Nicholas Yong has published two works of fiction with Marshall Cavendish: *Track Faults and Other Glitches (2016)* and *Land of the Meat Munchers* (2013). In his day job, Nicholas is a senior journalist with BBC News.